H. ANNE HENRY

Three Times Burned

The Remington Hart Series, Book Three

First edition

ISBN: 978-0-9981545-2-7

This book was professionally typeset on Reedsy. Find out more at reedsy.com

This one is for you, Mom, because I was always daydreaming instead of listening.

Chapter 1

I pulled both sides of my jacket together and zipped it against the bite of the autumn wind. Gabriel's Chevelle prowled the roads near Dove Creek and we rode with the windows down, enjoying the night air.

My partner turned onto a county road, changing our direction and causing a crosswind to blow through the open windows. A whiff of smoke tainted the clean scent of the country.

"Smell that?" I asked Gabe.

He pointed his nose toward the driver's side window. "Yeah," he confirmed. "Doesn't smell like a grassfire."

"Let's check it out."

I scanned the horizon for any sign of fire, but couldn't find the cause of the smoky scent on the breeze. The road curved off to the left, and Gabriel followed it.

"There it is," he said.

I tracked where his finger pointed out the window and spotted the robust red and gold flames, gray plume rising in silhouette against the dark sky.

As we approached, it became clear we were chasing a bonfire. A circle of headlights were pointed outward from the burning woodpile and young partiers crowded around to sit on tailgates or stand near the fire.

Gabe chuckled. "Brings back memories."

It was a Dove Creek tradition—like many small towns—to celebrate a football victory with a bonfire. A tradition I was surprised to see hadn't lapsed given recent events.

The entire town had almost been lost to a zombie attack only the month before, everyone living in or around Dove Creek becoming intimately familiar with our monster problem. We Amasai had also been outed, but so far left alone to go about our work in relative peace.

Though the scene revived happy memories for me, too, I knew the revelers weren't safe.

"Don't they know they're no better than vampire bait?"

"They're young and invincible," Gabe answered my rhetorical question. "Of course they don't care."

He slowed his car and cut the headlights as we got closer. There was enough cheap beer topping off red Solo cups that no one seemed to notice our approach. If they had any sense, they'd have posted a lookout for cops coming to bust them for underage drinking.

Better still, if they had any sense, they wouldn't be out there in the first place.

"We'll park over here and keep an eye on them," my partner said, putting the Chevelle in an inconspicuous spot.

"Good. I'll check in with Creed and Dylan," I told him.

When Gabriel cut the engine, I dialed Creed and lifted my phone to my ear.

"Hey sugar," Creed's smooth baritone came through the earpiece. "Everything okay?"

"All good here. We found a bunch of high schoolers partying

in a pasture, so we're gonna wait it out and make sure they don't become blood bags for the fang gang."

"Solid plan. Send us your coordinates in case there's trouble and we'll work our way over. Not much doing on this side of town."

"Will do," I agreed.

I switched to speaker phone to open the map function and set a pin at our location. Texting it to Creed and Dylan, I ensured they'd be able to drive right to us if things got out of hand.

"Got it," Creed said.

"Good. See you later."

He lowered his voice to a seductive purr. "Can't wait."

Dylan was in the background making gagging sounds and protesting about me being his sister before I disengaged the call. The exchange pulled a laugh from me.

Gabriel stared out the window and in the faint glow of the dashboard lights, I thought he looked a little green around the gills.

"You okay?"

He cleared his throat. "The smell of smoke is getting to me."

"Same here," I said, tucking my phone back into my pocket. "Let's roll the windows up. We'll be able to see anything from a mile away with that fire."

Gabe smiled and pressed the button to raise the glass. "You might."

It was true my vision enhancement courtesy of our guardian angel, Yescha, gave me an edge even in the dark. But, the glow surrounding the bonfire was bright enough where we sat, trouble couldn't hide for long.

"Do you love him?" Gabe asked.

I looked up from checking the magazine of my forty-five.

Not the kind of small talk I expected from my partner.

"I don't know yet," I gave him the honest answer.

"Guess I've always thought it's one of those things you know or you don't."

He had a point. With Dominic, I had known the moment I laid eyes on him. It had been a pull so powerful, otherworldly forces were at work, no doubt about it. We were destined for each other, so I had to wonder if my shot at forever was gone, taken by Valan as he took Dom's life.

There was no magic for me anymore. Shouldn't I make do with simply being happy instead of expecting to find forever again?

Sliding the mag back into the handgun, I shrugged. "I'm just... cautious. I mean, Creed and I make sense. We're good together, but..."

"But?"

I sidestepped what I realized was a rather sad way of looking at things, but stuck to the truth. "He doesn't know himself and it's a dangerous thing. Eden manipulated him into raising an entire graveyard. That's a lot of power in a loose cannon."

"You're not wrong," Gabe agreed.

"So, I like him a lot and I want to be with him, but talk of love just isn't in the cards right now."

Chambering a round, I flicked on the safety and holstered my backup weapon. One advantage of us becoming public knowledge was being able to use firearms with little worry. My trusty bow was still my demon-killing method of choice, but it was nice to know I could squeeze off a few rounds without drawing a crowd if things got dire.

"What about you?" I asked Gabe.

He glanced from the window to me. "Me?"

4

"Anybody special? I hear Suzie Levinson's been trying to get your attention."

Fresh off her second divorce, Suzanne Back-To-Her-Maiden-Name was like a rattlesnake with a brand new button on her tail. It was no wonder she was sniffing around an eligible bachelor like Gabriel.

He laughed. "Where did you hear that?"

"My brother, the gossip queen. Where else?"

"She's wasting her time."

Though I wanted to prod him for more details, the insistent, deep itch in my right leg distracted me. I winced and rubbed at my thigh where a zombie had bitten me during the fray. I had been thoroughly checked out and was cleared for duty weeks before, but the healing process was uncomfortable. Since they declared me out of danger, I had never gone back to Meredith for help.

Some wounds needed to heal in their own time.

"Is that still bothering you?" my partner asked, shooting me a sidelong glance.

"A little. You know how it is with deep wounds as they heal up."

"As long as it's normal lasting effects and not—"

"What? Something worse, like zombie cooties? Worried I'll go Walking Dead on you and try to eat your face?" I teased, trailing off into a show of rolling my eyes back and making screeching noises no live human should make.

Gabriel looked at me like an exasperated older brother would look at a ridiculous younger sibling, but busted out with a roar of laughter in spite of himself. The sound was infectious, and I laughed almost as hard, but a movement in the shadows across the road drew my attention and I sobered in an instant.

"We've got company," I told him.

No other words were needed. In unison, Gabe and I exited his car in near-silence. I ran around to his side, pulling an arrow from my quiver. We sprinted across the gravel road and I pointed to where I saw the approaching bloodsucker.

The crowd of teenage partiers heard nothing over the crackling of the fire and blaring country music. So focused on his prey was the vampire, he was oblivious to our counter-attack.

Sloppy, I thought. *Must be new.*

I watched as he looked behind himself, beckoning to another one of his kind. Catching Gabriel's eye, I held up two fingers.

He nodded once, then pointed toward me and motioned to the left. Pointing at himself, he then motioned forward. I gave a sharp nod to indicate I understood before taking off.

Flanking the pair of vampires, I cut them off from the pasture as my partner flushed them out. Like quail from their covey, the leeches scattered.

I let loose an arrow just as Gabe fired a bolt, both of us finding our targets with lethal accuracy. But we found the two vampires weren't alone in queuing to take a bite of young flesh. The firelight revealed half a dozen more of their kind.

My wrist went to my mouth, and I spoke into my smartwatch. "We need you *now*."

Though Creed and Dylan would already be on their way, they would have to step on it to be of any help. Ours weren't the only lives that depended on it.

There was a flurry of movement as the rest of the vampires came to realize what had happened to the first two. Half of them stood their ground as they recognized us as Amasai and prepared for a fight. The other three broke for the group of teenagers in an obvious bid for blood.

"Go!" Gabe yelled over the tumult.

A moment of hesitation took me—I didn't want to leave him to face the trio of walking leeches alone. But if I stuck with him, innocent lives would be taken.

I shot off after them, vaulting the barbed wire fence and following their trails through the coastal hay. As fast as I was, they had the advantage of speed and got out well ahead of me.

I knew the moment they reached the bonfire.

Music came to an abrupt silence, screams erupted, bodies scattered. It was like somebody had kicked over an antpile. If it hadn't been for my extra abilities, I wouldn't have been able to tell friend from foe.

I zeroed in on a male vamp who made a stout target. He grabbed a girl by the arm and dragged her, flailing and screaming, away from the chaos. No doubt thinking he was home free, he turned to sink his fangs into her and gave me a clear shot.

My arrow plowed into his back, finding its home in the unbeating heart. The body collapsed and the demon soul left a trail of crimson as it was pulled back to Perdition, but there was no disintegration. Just a heap of flesh and bone slumped on the ground with an arrow sticking up out of it.

The girl screamed before running blindly into the pasture. At least she'd be out of the way.

A deeper male shout ripped through the din behind me. I pivoted, nocking an arrow while seeking my next target.

The hayfield was a scramble of bodies fleeing, vehicles tearing out of their circled spots, and a whole lot of screaming and hollering.

A truck whizzed between me and the one I was aiming for, giving the bloodsucker time to bite the boy. In the chaos, the vampires had given up on the idea of dragging away their prey.

"Stop!" I yelled.

The vamp looked up at me, the bloody leer on his face questioning what I was going to do about it.

I let the arrow fly and the broadhead found eye socket. The shot wasn't enough to kill him, but he dropped the youth like a sack of dirty laundry.

"Go! Get out of here!" I waved the boy away as I ran toward them.

He clutched his bleeding neck, but scrambled to his feet and beat it.

The demon also fought to drag his carcass upright, but I was already waiting with another arrow. I hit him full in the chest with it, sending the hellspawn back where it belonged. Again, I was left with a fleshy heap instead of ash and dust, or even decay.

In the melee, I had lost sight of the third vampire I'd chased into the field. I searched the thinning crowd for it and my partner.

Gabriel was still fighting off two of the other trio, but was—

"Oof!"

The body hit me from behind, arms going around me in a tight grip. My bow was knocked from my hand and I struggled against the crushing hold.

"They warned us about you," the female voice told me.

The Holy Light within me surfaced, glowing and brightening until the bloodsucker relinquished her grip.

"You should've listened," I retorted.

She took a step back, looked for a moment like she would stand and fight, but ran instead. I tracked her while reaching down for my bow, but the sound of a gunshot rang out before I could draw. She dropped, and the demon energy that animated her fled back to Perdition.

I scanned the pasture for the source of the shot and found Creed at the edge of where the fire glowed. Jogging to meet him, I looked again to where Gabe had been struggling with his foes.

Dylan buried his axe deep in the back of the last vamp. It screeched and hissed, giving Gabe the opening he needed. He stabbed the heart with a stake, causing the body to wither as it should have.

Creed met me halfway across the battlefield and I sensed him giving me the once-over for injuries. I took a deep breath and my ribcage protested where the vamp I had tangled with squeezed me.

"I'm good," I told him. "A few bruised ribs, nothing major."

"Could've been worse," he said.

"It could always be worse."

I watched Gabriel wipe blood away from his mouth as he scanned the fallout. He spotted me and I raised a hand to signal I was okay.

The four of us converged near the fire, Gabe and I still catching our breath. As far as I could see, we were the only living things left in the pasture.

"Anybody get hurt?" Gabriel asked.

"One guy got bitten," I answered. "Best I could make out, his friends loaded him up and took off."

"Hope they took off for the hospital," Dylan said.

I pointed toward one of the felled vampires. "These didn't disintegrate."

"Only one of the three in the other group did," Gabe said. "Dylan and I will take care of them if you and Creed will double check for any victims we might have missed."

The silence after the uproar was deafening. Only the sounds of our boots crunching against the ground and the low crackle of the fire permeated the small hours of the night.

Gabe moved the first of the corpses with the power of his telekinesis. He concentrated and dropped it into the bonfire, and it went up like a stick of dry firewood.

Creed, Dylan, and I fanned out to walk the field to find the dead vamps and make sure we hadn't missed a human victim.

I came to the first bloodsucker I had shot, put my foot against his back, and freed my arrow. The broadhead was bent but Gabriel could re-forge it and the wooden shaft was still in good shape.

Bending down, I took a look at the body and found a fresh bite wound where his neck met his shoulder—a sure sign he had been bitten and turned recently. But I wasn't sure the bite was that of a vampire. It was far bigger than what a human mouth could do and even though the vamps had the added advantage of fangs, that didn't change the size of their chomper. The damage to the flesh looked closer to something like what a dog or wolf could do, but at last check, the werewolves weren't going around tasting people.

And thinking of Meg and Gio... I wondered where they had been. We could always count on their help in a fight, provided they sensed it. Had there been another attack elsewhere that night?

Dylan set fire to the female vampire that had gotten the drop on me, blue flames rising from the corpse as it burned to nothing.

"I've got one over here, Dyl," I called.

My brother joined me and he, too, noticed the bite mark.

"She had it, too," he told me, hooking his thumb back toward the burning body.

With Dove Creek Cemetery now empty, the demons' ample supply of dormant hosts was tapped. They were finding more uses for living humans than that of blood bag.

It made sense: Waste not, want not.

The bigger problem was the rate at which folks would be killed. As food, the living weren't needed but once every few weeks. But as hosts, someone would die each time a demon breeched our Plane.

If this kept up, the people of Dove Creek would near extinction soon.

"I think we'll find all the new ones that way," I said.

"We will," Creed said from behind us.

His expression was tight as he handed me the arrow he had plucked from the other vampire's skull.

Dylan lit the big male body and uprighted himself.

"Don't sweat it," he told Creed, clapping him on the shoulder. "We'll figure this out just like we do everything else."

I wished I was as sure of that as my brother and I wasn't the only one. Creed clearly had his doubts.

Short of finding and sealing the breech in the Planes, I wasn't sure what else we could do to prevent the demons from making more hosts.

Unless they didn't *need* more hosts...

Chapter 2

"You okay, sugar?" Creed interrupted my train of thought.

"Huh? Oh, yeah. Fine. What was it you said?"

"You're about to brew a pot of nothing but hot water," he pointed out.

I looked down at the coffeemaker and slid out the basket. Empty filter.

"Dammit," I muttered.

"Got something on your mind? You've been quiet since the bonfire."

Scooping coffee grounds into the filter, I started the maker and propped my hip against the kitchen counter.

"Yeah, I have an idea, or at least part of an idea. I'm not sure it's a good one… That's what I'm hung up on."

"Does it have anything to do with all the new hosts the vampires are taking?"

"It has everything to do with that."

Before I could elaborate, Dylan poked his head into the kitchen.

"Thought I smelled coffee," he grinned and walked all the way into the room. "Just came in from the armory. That vamp I axed left some bits of himself behind."

How my brother could be so buoyant after a night in the field and scrubbing vampire guts off his axe blade, I didn't know. I both loved him and envied him for it.

"Gabe's right behind me," he added as he took four mugs out of the cabinet. "He got pretty banged up."

"It's not that bad," Gabriel piped up when he appeared from around the corner.

I knew he'd gotten a busted lip, but in the light it was easy to see a blackening eye and a bruised cheek besides.

"I'll get you an ice pack," I said.

He made to wave me off, but I gave him a look that conveyed my lack of tolerance for an argument.

"You okay, Rem?" he asked as I rummaged in the freezer.

With Meredith's ability to heal injuries, we had little use for first aid. The ice packs had migrated to the back of the freezer behind tubs of Blue Bell and the frozen pizzas Aric likes.

"I'm fine," I said after fishing out Blue Ice from under Moollenium Crunch. "A few bruised ribs, that's all."

"You wanna call Meredith?" Creed asked.

"Nah, I wouldn't want her to waste the energy," I said.

"Same here," Gabe added. "Looks worse than it feels."

"That's good, 'cause it looks terrible," I told him, handing over the ice pack.

Creed handed me a cup of coffee and I sniffed it with an appreciation that never waned, no matter how many cups I sipped standing right there in that kitchen.

"Thank you," I smiled up at him.

He winked at me, and my insides went warm and fuzzy.

"Want to finish telling me your idea or wait til later?"

I heard the implied 'until we're alone' in his question, but considering my budding theory would affect how all the Amasai would operate, sharing was in the cards. Besides, my partner and my brother were the next ones I would've gone to.

I took a sip of the coffee he had made for me, paused, and stirred in some more creamer.

"Now's good," I said.

Dylan's ears pricked up like a hound on the trail, so I held up a hand to calm his enthusiasm.

"It's only an idea," I prefaced. "But with all the new victims from the demons taking new hosts—" Creed's face fell, and I reached out to touch his arm. "It's not a guilt-trip, it's just our reality now," I told him. "But every time we kill one, we're only sending them back to Hell on a temporary trip. When they were taking the dead from the cemetery, that at least kept them from feeding for a while, but now…"

"I think I know where you're going with this," Gabe said when I trailed off. "You might be on to something."

I nodded. "For every demon we send back, that's one more dead body when they're summoned again. So maybe we shouldn't send them back."

"And what? They just run free?" Dylan asked.

"No, we still fight them, keep them from feeding. Keep them contained. We injure them, but don't deal the death blow," I explained.

"It's a good idea," Gabriel said. "It'll work, at least for now. We'll need a more permanent solution."

"We find the breech and close it," I said.

"It can't be that simple. Haven't the Amasai been looking for it since your dad's day?" Creed pointed out.

"Not continuously," Gabe said, almost to himself. He was looking into the distance, not focused on any one thing. "They tried searching in the beginning, but decided their efforts were better spent expelling the demons. As Remi said, though, times have changed. We need to return to the Founders' original intent."

"And how do we do that?" Dylan asked. "Must be like looking for a needle in a haystack."

"It is. We'll have to be strategic. Even with our current numbers and extra help from Matt and Ty, we can't be everywhere at once. Let's think about it more and come up with a plan," I said.

Gabriel chuckled. "Never thought I'd hear you say those words."

Creed looked confused, and Dylan let him in on the joke. "In case you haven't noticed, 'think about it' and 'plan' aren't in my sister's vocabulary."

I swatted him. "Except they are. I just said them."

My brother made a face back at me, which drew a laugh from Creed. "If they're like this now, how bad were they as kids?"

"Have you met their mother? The woman should be nominated for sainthood when the time comes," Gabe said.

Creed gave me a pointed look. "I haven't had that pleasure yet."

Nor had I met his. With all of our respective parents living in Westview, we had no excuse apart from not making the time.

"I'll put in a good word," Dylan offered.

"Good man."

I rolled my eyes. "Now that's sorted out, I'm gonna go get some rest."

I drained my coffee mug and stuck it in the dishwasher. The others followed suit since the morning was getting away from us.

"Hugo is in the rotation tonight," Gabe said. "Let's come in a

15

little early and discuss your idea."

"Okay, yeah. Let's do that," I agreed.

The four of us filtered out of the kitchen and toward the front door. Garret was nowhere to be found, likely already gone to bed. I didn't blame him—I was ready to do the same.

I slid into the passenger seat of Creed's Escalade and buckled up. As soon as he shut his door and we were alone, I turned toward him.

"You have to stop blaming yourself for what the demons are doing. They're the ones killing people, not you," I told him as we left the driveway.

"They wouldn't be killing so many if I hadn't taken their hosts," he argued.

"And you wouldn't have taken them if Eden hadn't threatened to kill me. Look, we can talk this in circles all day, or we can try a new way of doing things and deal with what's in front of us instead of wishing it didn't happen."

Creed winced like I had slapped him. "Little harsh, don't you think?"

My rigid posture softened, and I changed my tone. "I spent a lot of time longing for different circumstances when Dominic was killed. It didn't change anything, only made me more miserable. Accept that a terrible thing has happened, then figure out what you can do to make it better."

Creed reached over and stroked my cheek. "Sometimes I forget how much you've been through."

"This isn't about me."

Creed swung his SUV into the spot next to my jeep and put it in park. The lot outside my apartment building was all but empty, everyone gone to work for the day.

I undid my seatbelt and shifted to look at him.

"What can I do to help you?" I asked. "Living in guilt is no way to live."

Creed shook his head. "I don't know. I keep thinking if only I can save enough lives, evict enough demons, I'll make up for my mistake. And now we know we've only been making it worse."

"We've all made mistakes along the way—"

"Any as spectacular as bringing down a zombie apocalypse on an entire town?"

"Well, no..."

"And there it is. I'm a freak, Remi. I tried to do something good, and it backfired."

"You are not a freak. You have a powerful gift—one you were given for a reason. We just have to learn what that reason is."

"You keep saying 'we,'" he pointed out.

"I'm here to help," I said. "But if you'd rather I butt out..."

"No. No, it's not that. I'm just still amazed you want to do this with me. It's not like I deserve it."

I reached out and smoothed his frown lines with my thumb. Taking his face in my hands, I kissed him.

"You're wrong."

"How do you know?" he asked.

I put the palm of my hand over his heart. "This, right here. It's full of good." I paused and gave his temple a gentle tap with my finger. "So stop overthinking with this."

Creed smiled and nodded.

The confident swagger, the infectious grin, the untouchable calm... All had disappeared with the zombie attack. I convinced myself all he needed was some time, but weeks had passed with little change. He was too in his head all the time, certain some horrible punishment was due him.

It was the old Creed I had fallen for, but I wasn't about to turn tail because he was changed by guilt he didn't need to shoulder.

What I had told Gabriel earlier in the night was true—Creed didn't know himself. It was at the root of his self-doubt and crushing guilt.

I couldn't steer him toward who he was, but I could help with what he was, and that was as good a place as any to start. It was time to go to Yescha. If anyone would be able to help us find the truth of Creed's origins, it was her.

"C'mon, let's go in," I told him. "I'll make us breakfast, then we can get some sleep."

Chapter 3

Not for the first time, I wished my dad was still around to ask him questions. From the time I had joined the Amasai, I had winnowed a few pointers out of him during our sporadic contact. He had mostly told me to learn from Hugo and trust him.

What I needed to know was how to get in touch with Yescha. How does one summon a guardian angel? Besides being in mortal danger or needing a divine power-up. The first, I couldn't trust. What if I took a swan dive off the nearest cliff, only to find it didn't merit divine intervention? And the second, I had already gotten—twice.

I rolled onto my back and stared at the ceiling. Next to me, Creed lifted his head and peered at me.

"Hey, sugar," he murmured.

"Hey. Sorry, I didn't mean to wake you."

"You didn't. Watchya thinking about?"

"You," I confessed. "I think Yescha could tell us about where your ability originates. She gave all of us Amasai our abilities. It stands to reason she might know about yours, or point us in the right direction, at least."

"It makes sense, but how do we communicate with her? And if we're able to, why would a guardian angel want to bother helping me?"

"She will. You're Amasai now and she told us it's her duty to help us when she can. But I don't know the answer to your first question, so that's the problem."

"Has she only come to you the times before?" he asked.

"Yes, she came the first time when she gave us our powers and helped defeat Apollyon. The second time, she summoned me to the Astral Plane. I would've expected her to show up for the zombies, but she had been distracted by something—"

"Did you say Astral Plane?"

"Yeah, it was weird. Like a dream, only not..." I trailed off when I realized what Creed was putting together. "Wait. That's where you go when you reanimate the dead."

"My consciousness. Which is probably what Yescha did when she summoned you there."

"Take us," I said. "You can take us to that Plane and we'll be able to find Yescha there."

"What? No, it's too dangerous. I won't risk your safety."

"I'll decide what risks I'm willing to take, thank you."

"Then you need to understand fully. Your spirit will be separated from your physical being. If something goes wrong, that separation could be permanent. Your body would die and your soul would be ripped apart, leaving you to wander as a ghost."

I propped my head up on my arm, undeterred. "Yeah, great. Thanks for that cheerful outlook."

"It's not that I'm undermining you deciding for yourself. If something happened to you while we're trying to uncover my origins, I'd never be able to live with myself."

"I get that and I understand the risk. But I've been to the Astral Plane once before and came back fine. Finding Yescha may be our only shot at getting some actual answers."

Creed closed his eyes, rubbed his face with his hand. "I'll think about it. I've never taken anyone with me before, so I need to consider how."

"Good," I smiled. "I'm sure you'll come up with something."

"Anybody ever tell you you're like a bloodhound on the scent when you've made up your mind about something?" Creed grinned at me.

I gave him a peck on the lips. "Not in so many words, but the word stubborn seems to get thrown around a lot. What are you up to tonight?"

"I'm on the graveyard shift at the downtown shop."

After the dust settled from the zombie attack, Creed had started working with the rest of us at the pawnshops. Since there hadn't been an opening for a steady spot in any one of them, he filled in wherever anybody needed some help in the schedule.

It was good for him. He was well liked by the others, and it kept him busy when he wasn't on Amasai duty.

"Well, that oughta give you plenty of time to come up with a plan," I told him. "I'm gonna go get ready since I need to get to HQ. Wanna grab an early dinner before I go?"

"Yeah, sugar. That sounds good."

I got out of bed and headed for the bathroom, but peeked back at him as I got to the doorway.

He had put a smile on his face when we were talking, but that had faded. Then, when he thought I wasn't looking, he stared at the ceiling like it had all the answers. He looked for all the world like a man in misery.

* * *

"So what you're saying is, we continue to defend people, but don't actually kill the vampires?" Hugo asked.

He, Aric, Gabriel, and I were in the armory getting ready for our shift on watch. I pulled on my jacket and made sure my throwing knives were in place.

"That's exactly what I'm saying," I confirmed. "If we injure them enough that they're incapacitated but the demon soul isn't released back to Hell, that's fewer people who get killed."

"I agree with your logic, *mija*," Hugo said as he sheathed his sword. "We'll need to keep a close eye on their numbers to make sure we're not giving them an opportunity to grow their ranks."

"And keep them on the defensive," Gabe added. "If they're constantly in recovery mode, there's not much they can do to increase."

"And we should look for the crossroads in the meantime," I added.

"As long as our efforts to do so don't interfere with protecting people, I'm all for it. I've been wanting to slam the door in the demons' faces for years," Hugo said.

"We have technology on our side now," Aric added. "It might be possible for Garret to set something up where we monitor activity, look for patterns."

"That's a great idea," Gabe said.

Not surprising in the least that my partner would cabbage onto that way of searching since it would be based on hard data. I smiled as I slid an arrow into the last gap in my quiver.

"Let's begin the strategy tonight, assuming we get the opportunity," Hugo said. "And we should be going."

He and Aric went back to the house so he could tell Meredith goodbye. Instead of going back inside, Gabe and I went straight around to the driveway.

"I'll drive tonight, if you want," I said.

"Be my guest."

We loaded into my truck and I fired up the engine. My jeep had gotten out of the shop a couple weeks before, and I thought about it sitting neglected in an extra spot at my apartment building. It and the big, green Ford had swapped places, and it was now my back-up.

I didn't need two vehicles, but the truck was paid off. God forbid I get into any more high-speed chases that end in shooting and flames.

When my partner settled himself into the passenger seat, it put the injured side of his face toward me. The swelling wasn't too noticeable, but the bruising had darkened more since that morning.

"How's your eye?" I asked as I put the truck in gear and pulled out of the driveway.

"Not too bad. Meredith offered to fix it earlier, but sometimes it's good to remember I'm just a normal human being. Not invincible."

"A normal human being who moves things with his mind," I smirked.

Gabe chuckled. "There's that."

I took the two-lane highway that went the short couple miles to Whitewing Lake. Our route would take us through the community on that side of the water and off to the southeast.

It was one of the prettiest parts of the county, with the knobby rock formations and gathering of oak and cedar trees. The only places we had that kind of thick vegetation were near water. I knew the oaks would be showing off their brightest colors at that time of year, though the headlights only allowed us to see glimpses of it. I made a mental note to take a drive during daylight hours.

The holiday season would start up later that week, which felt like the perfect time for romantic drives through beautiful scenery. Since I was putting the screws to Creed about going to the Astral Plane, a low key outing together seemed fitting to make up for the stress.

We hadn't made allowances in the rotation for a day of turkey and feasting that I knew of, so I glanced at Gabe and started the conversation.

"Any big plans for Thanksgiv—whoa!"

"Deer!"

The truck's brakes clamped down as I stepped hard on the pedal. We narrowly missed clipping the whitetail doe that came bounding out of the treeline and shot across to the next.

"That was close," I breathed.

"I thought we'd hit her for sure."

I applied the gas to get going again, but we got almost nowhere before a second animal blurred through in front of us. It was no deer, though.

Big and black, I would've sworn it was one of the werewolves if the color hadn't been all wrong.

"What the hell was that?" Gabe asked.

"Nothing good."

We looked across the cab at each other and were right on the same page: *Here we go again.*

About to ask my partner if we should get out and investigate, my question became moot before it left my mouth.

A second black beast tore out of the trees, but stopped to look at us. In the light of the high beams, it stared us down with red eyes. Teeth bared, we heard it snarl even over the patter of the engine.

It was warning us.

Then, as quickly as the beast had appeared, it streaked off into the same treeline where its twin had chased the deer.

We waited a moment to see if there were any more of the creatures, then Gabriel broke our stunned silence.

"Let's go check it out," he said. "We need to find out what that was."

He sounded like the very last thing he wanted to do was go after a pair of red-eyed monsters. In the dark. Through a claustrophobic grove of oaks.

I flipped a u-turn and parked the truck on the shoulder near where the ill-fated deer and her pursuers entered the wooded area.

"Send Hugo our coordinates. Just in case," I told Gabe as I got out.

In seconds, I had my quiver on my back and an arrow nocked. My partner pocketed his phone and loaded his crossbow. There was a light mounted on the frame and he switched it on.

"Ready?" he asked.

My brain had red-flagged the entire situation as one big Hell No, but we weren't leaving without answers.

"No. But let's go."

The leaves had only just begun to fall, but enough littered the ground that our every step was given away. I tried to tread lighter, but poise and stealth were Jocelyn's department.

To my right, the beam of Gabe's light swung slowly, carefully back and forth as he searched the trees. I didn't need a light, but the advantage of my eyesight was diminished since we couldn't see more than a few yards in front of us. But we kept moving, going forward even though our every instinct pushed us to go back.

25

Not far away, the howl of a wolf pierced the silence. An answering howl, more distant but still easily heard, quickly followed.

Gabriel turned his head and looked at me. The same question appeared to be running through his mind as was mine: How did those things get on Meg and Gio's radar?

In the quiet of the moment, we heard shuffling up ahead. I lifted my bow and drew back the string. My partner and I moved as one, our pace quickening with a destination now clear.

The shuffling sound became more distinct—legs working back and forth, scattering dry oak leaves. Hooves pawed at the ground, fighting to gain traction. A low growl rumbled like that of a prehistoric beast. There was a snarl in return and then... The shuffling sound ceased.

The trees opened into a small clearing and revealed a bloody scene. The odor that hit my nose was pungent and familiar. It was the same acrid stench from the pawnshop the night the Triple Six attacked. Like hundreds of burning matches... sulfur.

I tried to grasp just what it was I was looking at, but the creatures were like nothing I had seen before—and that's saying something.

They were like a hellish experiment gone wrong. A mastiff crossed with a dragon. All black except for those burning red eyes, their fur bristled like it was coarse and matted. They each had a mouthful of razor-sharp teeth that flashed ever time they went in for another bite. Claws that put the teeth to shame tipped paws the size of saucers.

I had only ever heard of their kind before and would rather have kept it that way: Hellhounds.

Deliberating about whether we should be the ones to make

the first move, I was blindsided by the vampire's approach. But across the clearing, he looked just as surprised to see us as we were to see him.

With my bow already drawn taut, I merely shifted my aim from the hellish canines to the vampire's heart. Recalling my idea that we had discussed with Hugo, reason overrode instinct and I recalibrated to shoot to wound, not kill.

In the fleeting moment, the demon began to beg for his life. "Lucifer, Lord of Perdition, save m—"

My arrow cut off his plea, though I didn't take the kill shot. The demon soul remained intact as the broadhead sliced into the abdomen instead of the heart.

The cacophony set off by the exchange left us no choice but to engage. The hounds had been content to ignore their demon dog walker and finish their meal, but our presence set them off.

I reached for another arrow as the beasts abandoned their kill and came for Gabe and me. Their strides were huge and they covered the distance in a flash.

Loosing the arrow I had at the ready, I was dumbstruck to see it hit my target but fall without doing any damage. The bristled fur acted as armor, the arrow unable to pierce it.

The hellhound was already upon me, so I gripped the frame of my bow and thrusted my left hand forward. The spike bit through the thinner fur at the jugular and the beast yelped. Its weight and momentum were too much for me, sending me to the ground on the flat of my back.

Jaws snapped mere millimeters from my face. I got a good look at where my bow's spike had wounded the beast, and the flesh sizzled, much how a vampire's reacted to silver.

With my hands gripping my bow to brace against the attack, I couldn't get to my knives. It was a stalemate my waning strength couldn't outlast.

Chancing a glance to the side to check on Gabriel, I saw him gain the upper hand and take the hellhound's back to cut its throat. Just as the hope he could help me was burgeoning, the beast bearing down on me was hit by an auburn freight train and toppled over. He rolled to his feet and rose with a snarl.

Meg faced off with the hound, hackles raised and lips peeled back over sharp teeth. Her interference gave me enough time to get my feet back under me. I snapped my bow into place on my back and drew the two silver daggers. My partner appeared on my other side, winded and with blood on his hands.

The remaining hellhound recognized how badly he was outnumbered and turned tail. Meg tore after him. Knowing Gabe and I wouldn't come close to keeping up, I looked for Gio and found him with a massive paw in the middle of the downed vampire's chest.

"Gio!" I got his attention. "We're okay here. Go with Meg."

Without hesitation, he left his post watching the bloodsucker and raced after Meg and the beast. I took his place and ran to the vampire I had shot. If I couldn't kill him, at least I could press him for some answers.

"What do you use them for?" I asked, referring to the hellhounds.

"Why should I tell you?" he fired back, though his voice was reedy from the pain.

The physical implications of being shot in the gut wouldn't affect him much, but he was being poisoned by the silver. His hands rested over where the shaft protruded from his host's non-vital organs, protecting the wound. I could still hear the sizzle of the flesh and smell the distinctive scent of a chemical burn.

"Because I'll leave you here to rot," I told him.

When he said nothing and looked at me with contempt, Gabriel reached down and gave the arrow a sharp twist. The leech wailed in agony as the broadhead sliced into new flesh, setting off a fresh round of sizzling.

I was both surprised and impressed with my partner's unexpected ruthlessness.

"Start talking," he ordered.

"Alright... alright," the vamp sputtered. "They're our procurers." He stopped, panted. "Since your friend emptied the cemetery and you all dispatched our hosts, we need new ones. The hounds mark them, bring them to us."

"Body snatchers," I muttered. "How many are there?"

Lupine howls carried on the night air, Meg and Gio celebrating their kill.

"Two fewer now," the vampire wheezed.

"A real answer. Now."

"*Idon'tknow*," he interrupted me in a rush, as if he expected more punishment for his reticence. "Maybe you should ask your old pal Valan. He knows."

I huffed. The thought of shaking down their ancient leader for answers was just too much.

"Why do you call him her old pal?" Gabe questioned.

"He's obsessed with her. She slipped his grip. More than once." A pained grunt punctuated his answer. "No one does that. And now she's a light-wielder..."

I glanced at Gabriel—he looked just as nonplussed as I felt.

"A what?" I asked.

"You possess the Holy Light. There hasn't been a human light-wielder for centuries."

"What does that mean?"

"You truly don't know? You're marked for death. A sacrifice."

"That can't be true," Gabriel insisted. "Yescha wouldn't do that to her."

"You're nothing to the angels. Pawns in their endless war."

"Enough," I said. "I won't listen to this."

I shoved my daggers back into their sheath and stalked away. Behind me, I heard Gabe stomp through the fallen leaves, then pause. I kept going without looking back.

"Wait! You said you wouldn't leave me here!" the wounded bloodsucker protested.

I had made no such promise. And I knew he had worse coming from Valan if the demon general found out he had talked. Not that I cared.

Chapter 4

I was near the edge of the woods when my partner caught up to me. He held the head of the hellhound he had killed by the matted fur.

"To show Hugo," he told me.

We reached my truck and he pitched the head into the bed. I offered him a bottle of water to rinse his hands.

"What did you do with the leech?" I asked.

"Nothing. Left him there."

When Gabriel was short on words, it meant he was mulling something over. He dried his hands and typed a text into his phone.

"I told Hugo we're good here and we'll meet back at HQ," he said.

"Do you think it's true?" I asked quietly.

"Honestly, I don't know. He had nothing to gain from lying."

"Except rattling me," I said.

I couldn't believe Yescha would place such a burden on me without telling the truth. *Wouldn't* believe it. But we had been interrupted and I hadn't seen her since.

It made my plan with Creed that much more urgent—now we both needed answers.

"Did it work?"

"I'm not sure," I admitted. "I've been a target for long enough that being told I'm destined to die doesn't really frighten me. But to be a sacrifice… For it not to be my choice any longer. I need answers."

I told Gabriel about my plan to have Creed take me to the Astral Plane. He listened, frowned, and picked a few leaves out of my hair from when I had been knocked down by the hellhound.

"Creed's right. It is dangerous," he finally said. "But not knowing either about his ability or about the light that Yescha gave you are bigger threats."

At least he understood where I was coming from, wanting to take a calculated risk. I opened the driver's side door to my truck.

"C'mon, let's get going," I said. I climbed inside while Gabe went around to the passenger side.

I pulled back onto the road and continued on about my plan. "He doesn't want to do it. He said he will, but I know I'm forcing his hand."

"Unless there's another way to make contact with Yescha, I don't see how there's a choice. Besides, what that vampire said back there changes things. If it's not just about himself, Creed will be more willing."

He had a point. Before, I was trying to convince Creed to take me along on an Astral journey simply to make the connection between him and Yescha. Now I needed his help for me, too. I hoped if he cared for me as much as he seemed to, that would tip the scale in my favor.

"I hope you're right."

"This is not at all how I expected tonight to go," Gabe commented as we passed the lake.

We were in the hours between late and early, so there was no one else around. There were a few porch lights left on here and there, but the landscape was otherwise dark. People had, for the most part, been leaving us alone to go about our business, but I was still glad the lion's share of our patrolling took place when people were out of the way.

"Tell me about it," I said. "Though I don't have expectations anymore. It's just prepare for the worst, hope for the best."

I pulled into the driveway of headquarters and parked behind Aric's Subaru. Hugo's truck was there, too, so we knew they were already inside waiting for us.

My partner grabbed the hellbeast's head from the back of the truck. As he lugged the massive thing inside, I noticed the same burning match odor as before.

"That thing reeks," I said.

"No kidding. The first thing I'm doing when we're done here is taking a shower."

Hugo and Meredith, Aric and Garret were in the sitting area when we went inside. Gabe plopped the severed head onto the tile floor, inciting a collective inhale.

Our leader leaned in for a closer look. "There are stories of these hellhounds, legends that go back generations. I never thought I'd see them with my own eyes."

"Are you both alright?" Meredith asked us.

"We got knocked around," Gabe answered. "Nothing serious."

"There were two of them, but Meg and Gio helped us," I said.

"How did you kill it?" Aric asked.

"Silver dagger. I cut its throat," Gabe said.

"Our arrows can't pierce the hide," I added.

We both explained about the vampire and how he appeared to be accompanying them. And we told the others what he said about the hounds acting as their body snatchers. Gabe paused and looked at me before going on, asking tacitly if I wanted to share what the vamp had to say about me.

I gave a minute head shake. It didn't seem right to worry the others about something that could prove to be empty words.

"It wouldn't be Dove Creek without something new to kill," Aric commented, passing a palm over the pointy green spikes of his mohawk.

"Could silver bullets work?" Garret asked quietly. "You said your arrows wouldn't pierce them, but a bullet should have enough velocity to do the job."

"That's a great idea. How many do we already have in inventory?" I asked Gabriel.

Since we hadn't carried firearms as part of our regular arsenal until recent days, silver rounds weren't something Gabe and Aric replenished on the regular.

"Enough to get us started. Aric and I can get to work right away casting more."

"I'm ready when you are," Aric said.

"It's close enough to dawn, we'll call it a night for our rounds," Hugo said. "Casey, Joss, Creed, and Dylan are on watch tonight. Let's make certain they're in the loop and armed properly."

Even though Hugo had declared an end to our patrolling for that shift, I decided to stay at headquarters at least until daybreak in case Garret caught something on the scanners. Gabe disappeared to take his shower, and Aric went to the kitchen to grab a Dr. Pepper and wait for him so they could get to work in the armory.

I was on my way to the same destination, only for coffee, when Hugo caught me and pulled me aside.

"What's on your mind, *mija*?"

"It's that obvious?"

"Obvious to me, yes. There's something you didn't want Gabriel to say."

"Only because I don't want to cause a stir if it's nothing."

I explained about what the bloodsucker had said under duress, both about myself and us being mere pawns. I had a target on my back, not only because of Valan, but one Yescha had put there.

"I'll do some research," Hugo said. "Perhaps I can dig up who this earlier 'light-wielder' was. It may tell us something."

"I'm going to ask Creed to take me to the Astral Plane to try to contact Yescha," I confessed. His expression changed to one of surprise and concern, so I dove in and explained more. "I already asked him, actually, but to ask her about his necromancer origins. Then that happened tonight, so I'm determined to convince him."

"I'm assuming if you're trying to talk him into it, he's reluctant to put you in peril. He's told you about the risk it poses to you?"

"Yes. It's why he doesn't want to take me."

Hugo nodded. "As long as you're going into it with your eyes wide open... It may be the only way for either of you to find the truth."

"I agree. Gabe and I talked about it some earlier, and so does he."

"He knows, then."

"Only him. I haven't told anybody else, mostly not to worry anyone. And there really hasn't been time. I just had the idea yesterday."

"When will you do it?"

"Today, with any luck."

Hugo took a deep breath and put a hand on my shoulder. "I

know I don't need to tell you to be careful, but please do. And tell me if there's any way I can be of help."

"Thank you. I will."

The sun was just breaking over the horizon when I went out to the armory. I put away my bow and quiver, along with all of my blades and stakes. I disarmed down to the forty-five I habitually carried and put everything in its allotted place.

Hearing the door open and shut behind me, I turned around expecting to see my partner, but was surprised to find Creed coming toward me. The moment he reached me, he scooped me up into his arms and held me tight.

"I'll do it, sugar. I'll take you to find Yescha."

I pulled back and looked into his eyes as soon as my feet hit the floor. "What brought this on?"

"Gabe caught me on my way in. He told me about the hellhounds, the vampire, all of it. I didn't want to put you in danger just for me, but if I can help you... I will."

I wrapped my arms around his neck and kissed him hard.

"He said you would. I should have known he was right."

"I'd do anything for you. Surely you know that."

If I acknowledged nothing else, he was always one to rectify his mistakes. I thought back to the zombie situation and how he pulled himself together at my behest. So, he'd do anything for me, except seek out the truth of his origins.

But it hit me—he was afraid.

He had hidden behind a desire to protect me, and I didn't doubt he wanted to, but it hadn't occurred to me until then that he might fear the unknown. And if he would overcome his fear every time I needed him...

I kissed him again, slower this time, relishing the soft press of his lips against mine. My hands went lower, palms resting on his chest, the heat of him making itself known even through his shirt.

We wouldn't be alone for long, and I didn't want to stop at making out in the armory.

"Let's get outta here," I said when I pulled back. "I need a shower, then more of that."

Creed's brilliant smile cut through the somber look he had worn. "I can handle that."

Chapter 5

The bedroom felt cold compared to the steamy bathroom when I stepped out with only a fluffy white towel wrapped around me. I had assumed Creed would be waiting and ready to warm me up, but that wasn't what I found.

He had gotten out of his work clothes and into a pair of jeans and a t-shirt. When I appeared in the doorway, he rose from sitting on the edge of my bed and came to me. Taking my face in his hands, he placed a gentle kiss on my lips.

"As much as I want to drop that towel and make all kinds of love to you, I think we should get our visit to Yescha over with first."

I shivered just as much from the suggestion in his velvety smooth baritone as the cool air on my bare skin. But there was no doubt in my mind he was right. Maybe just a small doubt, but business before pleasure, as the saying goes.

That didn't stop me from meeting his lips with a heated kiss and tossing my towel aside.

"Hold that thought," I told him before sauntering into my closet. "We're getting right back to that when we're done."

"Damn, sugar…"

It didn't take me long to throw on a pair of yoga pants and a tank top. I had little faith in what man-made weapons could do for me in the In-Between, so I didn't see the need to deck myself out like I normally would for action.

"Where should we do this?" I asked as I went back to the bedroom.

"On the bed."

I lifted an eyebrow and was about to make a pert remark about why I bothered to put clothes on when Creed chuckled softly.

"It's safest," he said. "I need you to be completely relaxed and you're a fall risk once we're out."

"Got it," I nodded.

I laid down on the bed on my pillow like I would to go to sleep. Creed settled in next to me, turned on his side, and opened his arms. Getting into his embrace felt like the most natural thing to do, so I followed his non-verbal queues without hesitation.

"There's no, you know, necromancer handbook or anything, so I'm just going by what feels right. This may not work," he told me.

"I trust you."

Creed smiled and kissed my forehead before gathering me to his chest and resting his cheek against my head.

"Now, clear your thoughts and relax as much as you can. I'm going to try to capture your consciousness and take it with mine."

I did as he said and cleared my mind—save the permeating sense of anticipation. After a few silent moments, though, I wondered when he was going to get the show on the road. For one thing, he wasn't chanting like when I'd encountered him in the graveyard.

"No incantations?" I asked.

39

"Shhh... Not when I'm not summoning spirits," he whispered. "Be patient."

Patience wasn't a virtue I had in spades, but if the occasion called for it...

Something shifted, like I had a severe case of vertigo. Everything else fell away. I was moving through time and space, but with no reference point to guide me.

Then I heard his voice.

Like a lighthouse on a stormy shore, Creed guided me.

"Remi, I'm here. Come to me."

I wasn't sure how, but it bound me to him. When I thought about it later, I realized it must have been similar to how he drew the wayward spirits, only to much different ends.

When I finally felt a sense of gravity return, I found myself in what looked like exactly the place Yescha had brought me to. This time, I had Creed's hand in mine, and I wasn't overwhelmed. I was there with my own purpose.

"Yescha," I called. Though I had no idea how sound carried in that Plane, I didn't feel I would need to yell. "Yescha, can you hear me?"

In the blink of an eye, the angel appeared before us.

Though nothing in her perfect countenance suggested she was surprised or perturbed at seeing me, she radiated concern.

"Remington? I should have known you would seek me out, but how have you come to—"

Her gaze had turned upon Creed, and the moment it did, she made a hissing sound. In a flash of movement, she had her long, thin blade pointed at his heart.

"Why do you bring this creature before me?" she demanded.

Without hesitation, I stepped between the angel and Creed.

"What do you mean 'creature?'"

"Spawn of Perdition," she spat.

Creed winced as though someone had slapped him. My eyes went wide.

"*What*? What is that supposed me mean?"

"You truly did not know," Yescha said. Her silver eyes went from me to Creed as she lowered her weapon. "Either of you."

"It's why we're here, or, at least part of why we're here. Creed is a necromancer. I thought you might be able to tell us why."

"He is Nephilim," she stated baldly.

I had heard the word before, but wasn't sure what it meant. Seemed like it was one of those biblical terms that was hush-hush. In other words, it didn't come up in any Sunday school lessons I knew of.

"I'm sorry—I'm what?" Creed asked.

"Born of a human and a fallen angel. Much of the bloodline has been diluted over the millennia, but for you to have the ability to call upon the dead... You must be the direct descendant of a Fallen." Yescha's tone became more patient as she spoke, but she was still wary of him.

"Creed has been helping us, but you might know that already," I told her.

"I have been occupied on many fronts and regret that I have not watched over you as well as I should. Does your light react to him, Remington?"

"Yes, but I've trained it not to."

All along, I had believed the light reacted out of my feelings of attraction to Creed. I never even considered it could be a warning. Either way, it seemed to serve as some sort of confirmation to Yescha.

"Your help to the Amasai is the only reason I refrain from slaying you where you stand," the angel told Creed.

She stood in silence for a moment and appeared to concentrate. It was just long enough that I was about to ask what was happening, but a diffuse golden light appeared behind her. It grew stronger until a tall male figure materialized.

Where Yescha was all silver and iridescence, her counterpart was gleaming gold. He, too, was perfection made manifest. Taller and powerfully built, I got the feeling he would have no trouble overpowering anyone who dared to cross him—and not just because of his physical strength. There was an aura about him, a glow much like Yescha's, that radiated divine power.

"This is Michael. Leader of our Order," Yescha said.

"Michael. As in, the archangel Michael?" I asked, pure skepticism coloring my tone.

His voice was placid, just like Yescha's, but with a deeper and more melodic intonation. "Is it so difficult to believe? You have encountered a demon prince. Why not an archangel?"

"Because I meet demons every day," I told him. "Can't say the same for you angels."

He didn't quite smile, but amusement showed itself in his golden eyes. "She is exactly what you have said, Yescha."

For a brief moment, both angels were silent, and it was apparent they were communicating with each other on some divine wavelength Creed and I weren't on. Despite not being privy to their telepathic conversation, I didn't find it hard to guess what they were discussing.

Michael finally addressed Creed aloud. "Step forward, if you will."

Creed did as he was asked and took a few paces toward Michael. Even at his height, he had to look up to meet the archangel in the eye.

Placing his palm on Creed's forehead, Michael bowed his

head and closed his eyes. He stood that way for about half a minute, with me watching closely for any sign he was hurting him.

"Son of Azazel," he pronounced. There was a flash of enmity in his golden gaze before his expression reverted to neutral. "You are as Yescha suspected: Nephilim. But for your help to our human allies, your life shall be spared."

Creed was stone cold silent. I looked at him and watched to see if he was even breathing. His olive complexion went pallid, and he wiped his palms on the front of his jeans.

"My father was... Azazel?" he finally asked, as though struggling to get his head around the revelation.

Truth be told, I was, too.

"Is—he still lives. My brothers and I cast him out ourselves. Rafael imprisoned him, but he escaped some centuries ago."

I gasped. It was obvious he would be on the loose in order to sire children, but what was to be done about it?

Yescha interrupted my mental panic. "You have nothing to fear from him. Azazel rather likes mortals. His infatuation with your kind ultimately led to his fall."

While that information put me more at ease, Creed still looked like he was trying to recall the square root of pi. But after thirty years of not knowing your biological father only to be told he's a fallen angel? It was no wonder he had been hesitant to go digging for answers.

"We must not tarry in this place," Michael said.

"Wait. I need to speak with Yescha more. About the Holy Light," I said.

Michael looked at Creed. "You can see yourself back to the proper Plane?"

"Yes, but—"

"I will send her back safely," Yescha assured.

Creed's eyes met mine, looking for affirmation. I nodded once. He took a few steps back, then vanished into the ether. I hoped in the few minutes he would be left alone he wouldn't stew too much. We had a lot to discuss.

"You must part from him," Yescha said the moment he was gone.

"What? No," I said. It was a blunt response, but I had no intention of leaving Creed just because of his parentage.

"We have no quarrel with him, but his kind are outcasts. Nephilim are of neither Heaven nor Hell; they are of the Earth and, therefore, unpredictable. His father is an especially cunning and beguiling creature," Michael warned.

"That explains a lot," I said under my breath.

The apple didn't fall far from the tree in the charm department.

"Listen," I said more directly. "I'm not saying we haven't had our issues." Helloooo zombie apocalypse. "But Creed is loyal to us and he's been hunting vampires for years. I'm not gonna kick him to the curb because a father he doesn't even know can't color inside the lines."

"Obstinate, foolish girl," Michael pronounced.

I squared my shoulders. "I've been called worse."

"You said Creed was only part of the reason you came herein," Yescha reminded me.

"Yes, right. The last time we met, when you gave me the light, we were interrupted. I've figured out how to control it—mostly. But what does it mean in the grand scheme of things?"

I thought of Valan and his sincere shock at seeing the light within me. The vampire the night before had declared me marked for death. There had to be a good explanation for why this Holy Light thing was such a big deal.

Yescha looked at Michael before addressing me, as though seeking his approval.

"Holy gifts can only be given to mortals in certain circumstances. Your family has proven their loyalty time and again, and your father's sacrifice made it possible. Your brother is a fire-wielder and you are a light-wielder; powerful weapons against the demons."

"I was told last night that I'm a sacrifice, that I'm bound for death because I'm a light-wielder."

"It is true the last mortal to possess the Holy Light died while fighting for our side," Michael said. "But to call her a sacrifice is not accurate."

"What a relief," I said pointedly. It reminded me of what else the bloodsucker had said. "So it's as simple as that—we fight and die like the pawns on a chessboard while you angels stand back with all your sparkle and immortality and watch it happen."

"There are old agreements and vows in place that prevent us from interfering in certain situations. We call it the Balance. Yescha was able to come to your aid when Apollyon was summoned because none of you could oppose him."

"And Valan—one of us is a match for him?" I questioned.

"Yes. You, Hugo, Gabriel… You each posses the ability to defeat him."

I recalled my last altercation with Valan and though I hadn't been able to deal the death blow, he hadn't walked away in one piece like before. He was like any other vampire—all it would take to end him was a stake through his heart. But he was more cunning than the others, and I had an inkling the angels weren't coughing up all the details.

Maybe we weren't just pawns—if their hands were tied, it

made sense for them to work through us—but we also weren't on equal footing. Not like true allies. Much like the pawns, we couldn't see the entire playing field.

But there was one way we could level it.

"We're going to find the Crossroads and close the breech," I told them.

"You already know where it is," Yescha said. "You do not realize it, but the place is familiar to you."

Not exactly a helpful detail since that could still be anywhere in Dove Creek.

"Any helpful hints on how to close the door and lock it?"

"You have every necessary tool at your disposal to close the gates," Michael said.

"Work with the light; it will do as you command. Your mind is the only limitation," Yescha told me.

They were still talking in half-truths and riddles, but I felt they were trying to help. And I obviously had their blessing to shut down our Crossroads, which was a relief. I still had my doubts, though I had gotten more out of our visit than I had hoped for.

"I will," I told Yescha. "I've been here longer than I was last time. It's time for me to be getting back."

"Yes, you should not linger here," Michael agreed. "It was a pleasure to meet you, Remington. I do hope you succeed."

With that, he evaporated into a golden cloud and faded away.

"Please consider what we have asked of you regarding Creed," Yescha reminded me. When I opened my mouth to tell her no dice, she lifted an elegant hand to stop me. "Consider it, absent your feelings for him. Until we meet again, Remington."

Yescha touched the tips of her fingers to my forehead and there was a moment where I lost all sense of time. But the journey out of the Astral Plane was much less of a bumpy ride than the trip into it had been.

I sat straight up in my bed, as though jolted awake from a dream. Creed was pacing my bedroom and came to my side the second he heard me stir.

"Remi, thank God," he breathed. He gathered me into his arms. "I was worried sick."

Chapter 6

"What do you mean?" I asked, confused. "I was gone only a few minutes longer than you."

Creed pulled back but didn't let go of me. "It was hours on this side. Time moves differently between the Planes."

I frowned, trying to work out how a handful of moments in the Astral Plane translated to hours in the Mortal Plane. Reaching for my phone on the nightstand, I checked the time. Sure enough, it was late in the afternoon.

"That's crazy..." I muttered.

Oddly, even though the entire day was gone and I'd had what seemed like half an hour of a flurry of activity, I felt well-rested. I arched my back and moved around a bit, stretching like I would have after waking from a good night's sleep.

I hadn't technically slept, but the info I had gotten from the angels was as satisfying as a full day of shut-eye.

"What else did they tell you after I left?" Creed asked.

"I asked Yescha about the light and about what that vampire said last night." Only last night—it felt like an eon already. "And I asked about the Crossroads. I didn't get many answers on that score, but at least I was able to get some reassurance that I'm not gonna snuff it based on being a light-wielder alone."

I was deliberate in leaving out the part where Yescha and

Michael had urged me to break up with him. I had no intention of kicking him to the curb, so what he didn't know in this case wouldn't hurt him.

He wrapped me in another tight embrace. "Good. That's great news."

"The thing is, we have a fight ahead of us. I may not be an intentional sacrifice, but I'm not completely in the clear," I cautioned. "What about you?" I changed the subject. "Now that you know who your father is…"

"Honestly? I don't know where I'm at with it," he admitted. "I've had all day for the shock to wear off, so I guess I'm relieved just to know. But it feels weird to have a label to put on me… Nephilim… It still doesn't tell me much about what I am."

"But it gives us somewhere to start. We can research, find out more about others like you."

"The angels weren't too keen on you hanging around me."

My shielding him from the truth hadn't prevented him from seeing it for himself.

"So what? You'll notice they didn't say you're irredeemable. You can't be condemned for the sins of your father and you've shown us your true character. That's all I care about."

Creed smiled. "I still can't believe you stepped in front of an angel's sword for me."

"It's no different from when we're in the field. I won't sit back and watch while someone I care about is threatened—not even by an angel."

Yescha hadn't been completely out of line based solely on what she knew of Creed's kind, but tensions had needed to be taken down a notch. I had done the only thing I knew in the moment would get her attention.

"Besides, I had dragged you there," I continued. "Wouldn't be fair to just serve you up to be skewered."

I smiled and tried to make light of it. There was nothing easy about learning Creed was the son of a Fallen, but I imagined it was a thousand times harder on him, no matter how good a face he was putting on.

"I'm glad we both made it out alive," he said. "Thank you for making me go."

He moved in closer and eased into a lengthy kiss. Whether it was sheer relief that I returned safely or the need to reconnect after our encounter with the angels that drove his desire, I didn't care. Our focus had been on hellhounds and survival and questions of such gravity that we hadn't taken enough time to simply be together. As his hands moved over my skin, I found I craved his touch—I hadn't had enough of it.

The yoga pants and tank top I had put on after my shower made an unnecessary barrier to that touch, and I couldn't get them off fast enough. Creed yanked his t-shirt off and cast it to the floor before recapturing my lips with his own. One of his hands went to my hair, his fingertips sending tingles across my scalp and down my entire body. He pulled just hard enough to expose my throat. The stubble on his jawline scratched against the delicate skin on my neck, my shoulder, my collarbone… more, as he left hungry kisses behind greedy hands. And just like coming and going from the Astral Plane, I lost all sense of time. I forgot everything but him.

* * *

Since I was on backup duty that night, Creed and I rode to headquarters together. He pulled into a spot behind Casey's Bronco and put it in park.

"Will you tell Hugo?" I asked.

"Yeah, tonight, since he's not here. I'll talk to Dylan first while we're on the road, then call Hugo."

He still gripped the steering wheel, white-knuckling it while he laid out his plan. It wasn't as easy as he was making it sound.

"After that, I'll let it come out naturally. I don't wanna make it into some big thing, you know?"

"Yeah, I gotcha," I told him.

I understood his reasoning. It'd be extra awkward to stand in front of the group and explain that his father was a fallen angel. And not only a Fallen, but one who invited the animosity of the Archangels themselves. No matter how accepting the others were, it would be uncomfortable.

Reaching over, I took one of his hands off the wheel and held it in both of mine. I brushed my lips across the backs of his knuckles.

"It's going to be fine," I said. "I'm with you. I know the others will be, too."

"I hope you're right."

His answering smile was a sad one as he placed a warm palm against my cheek. He kissed me softly and stroked his thumb across my cheekbone.

"We'd better get inside. Dylan will be waiting for me," he murmured.

"Let him wait," I purred and pressed my lips to his.

My brazenness drew an honest to goodness laugh from somewhere deep in his chest and put a twinkle back in his eye.

"You know how he is if he's kept waiting."

"True," I winked. "But I expect to continue that in the morning."

"Your expectations won't be disappointed."

Since I had nearly made him late, Creed went straight around back to the armory. I went into the main house and stopped to say hi to Garret.

"How's it going?"

He adjusted his thick black glasses. "Well, I'm working out the final kinks in a program that will help us track vampire activity."

"That's amazing—I didn't expect you to get it done so quickly."

"It's a simple program, really. A mapping system. And Stacey lent a hand with some of the features. I don't know why I never thought of it myself."

He deflected my praise in that diffident way he had, but we all knew who the technological guru was, no matter what he said to diminish his natural capabilities.

"We didn't think it was a need until now," I shrugged.

"The good news is, I can include historical data. Coordinates from the times you guys called in or texted. I've logged it all. I'm hoping to crunch the stats later tonight."

"Even better," I told him. "I'll get out of your hair in that case. Be in the armory if you need me."

The four on watch that night were already armed and ready to hit the road when I got out there. I was their backup, the only one since it was Sunday night and it was easier for the others to be off.

On his way out the door, Creed paused to pass me his keys and plant a kiss on my lips.

"I know I don't need to tell you to be safe out there," I told him.

"You don't. I will," he smiled.

"Call me if you need me."

I exchanged greetings and goodbyes with my brother, Joss, and Casey as they made their way out. They all had fair warning about the hellhounds along with silver bullets in their guns, but I still hoped they'd be spared a run-in. Better still, maybe we'd be lucky enough the pair from the night before were the only ones. I doubted the thought the moment it crossed my mind, but it was a pleasant one to entertain.

Even though I had come to the armory to get my gear and be at the ready, Yescha's advice to work with the light stuck with me. Instead of trading my lead bullets for silver as I had intended, I stopped in the center of the expansive room. It felt odd, standing all alone in the quiet, but the feeling of silliness quickly faded as I concentrated on the power within me.

There were some ways in which I had gained control of it already. For one, I didn't light up like a Christmas tree every time Creed touched me. But I could also channel it from being the all-over glow to focusing it in one place, like my hand.

I thought of how Dylan could cast fireballs from his hands. If I could somehow focus the light, create an orb or even a beam…

The surge welled up from deep within, and I captured it. Directed it to my left arm. The glow traveled down to my hand, and I opened my fingers. Brighter… brighter… The pure white light gathered until it shone more brilliantly than I had seen yet.

I lifted my hand and tried to project the light outward. It flared in its brilliance, but never traveled past my fingertips. The exertion had my chest pumping with deep breaths and I dropped my arm, the light going dim as I did.

My shoulders slumped with my frustration. It was only the first try, though. I caught my breath and recalled Yescha's words: *Work with the light. It will do as you command.*

53

Focusing anew, I sent the light into my left arm again. As if sensing what I wanted it to do, it gathered more quickly this time. I raised my hand to shoulder height, this time with my palm up, so I could see what was happening.

Again, the light flared in intensity. I concentrated all my efforts on projecting it out of my hand and into an orb. It flickered white and came out just past my fingertips. I curved my fingers to capture it, but couldn't move it past where it was.

My breath heaved with the exertion. I pushed past what I thought was my limit, but still no payoff.

Determined, I shed my jacket and tossed it on a workbench.

This time, the light glowed in my left arm with only a single thought. My focus was laser-beam accurate and the light and I worked together, moving past the struggle. Something surged within me, a dam breaking. It no longer felt like the Holy Light and I were separate beings.

I held my hand up in front of me and watched with awe as the light did exactly what I wanted. Re-centering, I wrapped the beams in my hand around themselves until I held a perfect ball of the white glow.

Pointing my palm away, I sent the orb flying just as the armory door opened. The light struck the doorway only inches from Gabriel, yanking surprised sounds from both of us.

"Gabe!" My hands flew to my mouth and my eyes flared wide.

The white light clung to where it had hit, then dissolved into nothing. It didn't leave behind so much as a mark.

I rushed toward my partner. "I'm so sorry… I was working on controlling it and didn't expect anyone to come in."

"Don't worry about it. No harm done. How was it coming before I interrupted?"

Shrugging my shoulders, I huffed a little. "Frustrating. But

I've made a lot of progress just tonight. I really should've been doing this all along, but I thought the light just sort of did what it wanted... So, what are you doing here? I thought you had the night off."

"I do. I wanted to check on you, though, and put in some extra time out here."

Eyeing his dressy clothes, I was dubious. He had on charcoal gray slacks and a black dress shirt, and, knowing Gabe, there had probably been a tie involved at some point. Hardly attire for casting silver bullets.

"You look awfully nice for working out here," I told him exactly what I was thinking.

"Well, I had a date," he said.

I checked my watch—not even ten o'clock.

"Did she have a curfew?" I teased.

Gabriel laughed. "No... I cut it short and dropped her off after dinner. She just wasn't my type."

I shrugged. "It happens. I didn't know you were back in the dating pool after what you said about Suzie Levinson the other night. Wait," I stopped, pointed a finger at him. "The date wasn't with Suzie, was it?"

Bigger laugh. "No way. That has pre-nup written all over it. Not looking to be her next ex-husband."

I laughed so hard I had to clutch my sides. "I should tell you how wrong that is, but you're totally right."

After the side-splitting giggle, I caught my breath. "Want any help? I've got all night, obviously."

"I'd love some. Aric's working, otherwise he'd be here."

"Speaking of working, don't you have to tomorrow?"

Gabe unbuttoned his cuffs and rolled them up. "I do, but no early meetings and I didn't feel like going home yet. So, now you're fussing over my schedule?" he asked with a smile.

"It's only fair since you nag me over how much sleep I get."

"True."

We went to the long work table and bench that spanned most of one side wall of the armory. There were three sets of molds full of the casings he and Aric had cast in the early morning hours.

"I'm doing one caliber at a time to stay organized. These are forties, since that's what all of us use most," Gabriel explained.

I nodded to show I understood. "Let's remind everyone to be judicious with their aim since this isn't a quick process."

"All too true." Gabe popped the top on one of the molds to reveal 100 pristine silver .40-caliber casings.

"So what can I help with?" I asked.

"At this stage, keeping me company," my partner chuckled. "This part's tedious. I've got to get the exact amount of powder in each one of these. Too much and—"

"Bigger bang than we bargained for," I supplied.

"Yeah, that."

Gabe handed me a pair of clear safety glasses. "Your eyes are the most important we've got."

"The sharpest. I dunno about most important," I said, sliding them on.

Putting on his own pair, Gabriel reached for a canister of gunpowder. He collected a measuring cup and a tiny funnel and got to work. He was right—it was the kind of fiddly, detailed labor that would get monotonous all too quickly.

"Did you stop and talk to Garret on your way in?" I asked, breaking the silence.

"No, I came straight out here," he answered without missing a beat. "Why?"

"He's almost done with a program to document vampire activity. He said it'll process our historical data, too."

"Excellent. It'll be good to start with some hot spots instead of just throwing darts at the map blindfolded."

"Agreed. But I have to wonder if we'll know it when we find it," I paused. I hadn't told him about Yescha and Michael, or any of it. "Yescha said it's a place I'm already familiar with, but she's forbidden from telling me exactly where. Something about the Balance."

I made air quotes when I said it. The whole concept of keeping a balance of power between Heaven and Hell was utter bullshit to me.

Just duke it out already. Winner takes all.

"So you did go. I wondered when you didn't say anything."

"I was getting around to it. Besides, I think I have you to thank for it since whatever you said to Creed convinced him to take me. He said he'd do anything if it was for me."

"He's not the only one," Gabriel murmured. I started to ask what he meant, but he moved on briskly. "Don't thank me unless it was good news. Was it?"

"Mixed bag. I met an Archangel, which was interesting."

"Seriously?" he asked, sounding more awed than I felt. "Which one?"

"Not your namesake. The other one—Michael."

"Wow. How was that?"

"Like I said... interesting. He was a lot like Yescha, only bigger and very... gold. Anyway, they told us about Creed's origins." I paused and had a brief internal debate about whether to tell my partner, but decided to in the end. Creed already knew I talked to Gabe about everything. He had to have guessed I'd spill the tea if I saw him that night. "He's a Nephilim. They weren't too happy about it, but seeing as how he's been helping us—"

"Wait, slow down," he interrupted and looked up from his work. "Creed's a Nephilim?"

"You know what that is?"

"Of course. You don't? I thought your degree was in World History?"

"Yeah, World History. Not biblical apocrypha."

Gabriel ignored my sarcasm. "How many generations is he removed from the Fallen who sired his line?"

"His line? What do you...? None. No generations—he's the son of Azazel."

Passing a hand over his freshly shaven face, he blew out a breath. "That's a big one, Rem."

"I know. Or, at least I think I know. Bad big?"

"Not necessarily. We've known Creed for months now. Knowing who his father is doesn't suddenly change who he is."

I told Gabe about the rest of our talk with the angels, about how they sent Creed away and we talked about the breech, and Yescha telling me to work with the light. I left out the part where they had urged me to leave Creed. Since I hadn't told him myself, I didn't want to risk him finding out by accident. And I didn't want to poison the well.

"On the positive side, now we have something to go on to find the Crossroads, and we know you're not destined for the grave just because of the Holy Light," Gabe said. "What will Creed do about his news?"

"He said he was going to tell Dylan tonight. Since they've been partnered up, it made sense to out it to him first. Then, he was planning to call Hugo."

I glanced at my watch again. If he had told both Dylan and

Hugo, I would have expected to hear from him by then. I hoped it didn't mean trouble, either of the disagreement type or the vampire type.

"And after that?" Gabe prompted.

"Just let it come out naturally—no big announcement. I mean, it won't come as any surprise that I've told you. And you know how Dylan is."

"He's worried about how we'll react," he commented.

"A little, but mostly he doesn't want to make a big fuss."

My partner went back to meticulously filling silver casings. "Not a big fuss, but it'll be something to talk about. Speaking of talking... I'm glad you trust me now when there's something going on instead of trying to do everything yourself."

"There were a lot of things that happened, specifically Dylan getting kidnapped, that showed me I was bull-headed in thinking I needed to handle everything on my own."

"You wouldn't be who you are if you weren't bull-headed," he said, the corners of his lips turning up.

I grinned and gave him a light slap on the shoulder. "I'm serious. I can't do any of this without you, but I think you know that."

Pausing his work to look up at me, Gabe grew serious. "That's not true, Rem. You're capable of doing anything you decide to do and you don't need me. But everybody needs help sometimes, and I'm here for those times... Anything you need."

"That goes both ways, you know."

Gabriel nodded once and didn't break eye contact. "I do... I do know."

I was taken back to the time when we had fought Valan at Creek Crossing, and I had confessed to caring about him. Standing in the rain, I made my feelings known, but he had

59

let the moment grow awkward. Probably because he cared about me no more than a partner in the field should and now, thankfully, a best friend.

We were saved from any awkwardness this go-round by my phone beeping a text alert.

I slid it out of my back pocket and pulled up the message from Creed.

TALKED TO DYLAN AND HUGO.
BOTH COOL.

"It's Creed," I told Gabe. "He talked to Dylan and Hugo and they were good about it."

He had already resumed his task. "That's good. I'm glad."

I quickly sent a reply:

TOLD YOU SO.
I TOLD GABE.
HE'S COOL, TOO.

I put my phone back in my pocket and watched Gabriel for a moment. He was already halfway through the last tray, despite all the talking we had done.

"I started to ask you last night if you have plans for Thanksgiving, but we were interrupted," I said.

"Right. That's this week, huh?"

"Yup," I confirmed.

"My sister Gwen is hosting dinner at her place. I just have to show up and eat."

Gwen was the Wyatt sibling who was my age. A feminine version of Gabriel, she was blonde-haired, blue-eyed perfection. But unlike her older brother, she didn't so much appreciate the finer things in life as demand them. Not long after graduation, she had caught her a surgeon nearly two decades older and set herself up as a trophy wife. These days, they lived in a boujie subdivision in Fort Worth that made the houses in Iron Terrace look like tiki huts.

"Are you staying the night?" I asked. "We can cover a few nights for you in the rotation if you want to take off."

"No, I'm going straight there and back. It's not that far and I find spending too much time with my family... taxing."

I giggled. "Well put."

"Thanks, though. Any big plans for you?"

"Nothing big. My mom invited us over, Dylan and Joss, too. She invited James, but he politely declined. I guess he finds us taxing."

Gabe and I had a good laugh as we fell back into our normal rhythm. I was able to give him some actual help when it came time to close the casings, and within another hour, we had a few hundred rounds more to work with. I kicked him out to go get some sleep before work and went back to the main house to wait out sunrise.

Working on the silver ammunition was the most action I saw all night. Not that I was complaining.

Chapter 7

"Too quiet last night," Creed commented as he drove us back home in the early morning light.

"It just feels that way after how much happened the last couple days."

He glanced at me sidelong and smiled. "Hope you're right."

Turning into the parking lot for my building, Creed eased into the spot next to my truck. He came around to open my door for me and took my hand when I got out.

"It's a relief the others reacted the way they did when we told them about my father," he said.

When they had come back to HQ, we made quick work of talking to Jocelyn, Casey, and Garret. They felt about it much the same as Gabriel—it changed nothing as long as Creed was on our side.

I knew over the course of the morning Garret would tell Aric, and Hugo had either already mentioned it to Meredith or would. She would be as unfazed by it as she was by anything else, so that would be that. Every Amasai would know we had a Nephilim on our team and we'd go about our business as usual.

"You hafta give us more credit," I told him. "A family doesn't turn its back on one of their own, especially not over something you can't change."

We reached the base of the stairs that led to my second-floor apartment, and I caught a whiff of tainted air. My skin prickled as I came to an abrupt halt.

"What is it, su—"

"Wait," I said, reaching for my handgun. "Smell that?"

Creed sniffed the cool morning air. "Yeah, it's awful. What is that?"

Burning sulfur. I wasn't mistaken.

"Hellhound. Gabe and I smelled it the other night," I told him. "You armed? Silver bullets?"

He nodded. "Yeah, I have my Sig."

"Good. Split up and go around the building. You go left."

I ran to the right, across the front of my building and toward the breezeway that separated it from the next. We were approaching that time of morning when a steady stream of residents would come from the apartments as they all headed to work and school. It would be all too easy for a hellbeast to snatch an unsuspecting victim.

The farther I moved in that direction, the less I smelled the hellhound's distinctive odor. Which meant...

I turned on a dime and raced back in the direction Creed had gone. He had already rounded the other side of the building when I heard his voice.

"Remi!"

With everything I had, I sprinted to where his cry had sounded. Handgun leveled, I came around the building and found the hellhound on Creed, his arm between its powerful jaws. He was struggling to fight off the beast.

I aimed and double-tapped the trigger. Two silver bullets pierced the hound's skull, and it fell into a heap on top of Creed. I let out a heavy exhale and ran the rest of the way to help him.

Creed heaved the carcass off him and struggled to get to his feet. I put a hand under his uninjured arm and helped him up.

"It got the drop on me," he said, clutching his left arm. "I never even got a shot off."

"I'm sorry—we shouldn't have split up. Are you okay?"

"No, it was the right call. We needed to find that thing fast." He paused and made a ginger movement with his arm. "I'm pretty sure it's broken. Would've been worse without a jacket on. Those teeth are legit."

People appeared at their doors and on balconies to check on the commotion. They were tentative, as they should have been after hearing gunshots, but we had an audience, nonetheless.

"How are we gonna get rid of this thing?"

"I have an idea," I told him.

Focusing, just as I had in the armory hours before, I directed the Holy Light to my left arm. I pointed my palm at the dead hellbeast and hit it with a beam of light. The mass of matted fur and snapping jaws disintegrated into white embers and black ash. It sparked and withered until there was nothing left.

I could just make out the sound of concerned murmurs from the people watching. After the zombie attack forced the entire town to take a good, hard look at the supernatural goings-on, this would come as no big surprise. It wasn't difficult to imagine their questions, though.

Starting with: What the hell was *that*?

"Is it safe now?" one woman's voice called, loud and clear. "Can we come out?"

"All clear," Creed answered calmly.

To our surprise, a few "thank-yous" were spoken before folks went about their business.

"I didn't know you could do that," Creed said, pointing at the spot where the hellhound had disappeared.

I shook my head. "I didn't, either, until last night. Even then, I wasn't sure that would work."

"Glad it did. I don't think Animal Control would've been happy to get the call for disposal of that."

"Let's get inside. I'll call Meredith and ask her to come look at your arm."

She told me my timing was impeccable because she had just left the drop-off line at school. It would be a few minutes, so I offered to have coffee ready and waiting.

We hung up, and I texted Solomon in case Creek County Sheriff's Department got any calls about the ruckus with the hellhound. The detective would be able to head off any issues.

THX FOR THE HEADS UP.

LET YOU KNOW IF I NEED ANYTHING.

He replied as I was filling a filter with coffee grounds.

"Are you hungry?" I asked Creed. "I could make us something more than coffee."

"No, thanks. I think I still have a little too much adrenaline pumping," he smiled.

I didn't want to go through the bother of making breakfast just for myself, so I snagged a cereal bar from the pantry to have with my coffee.

The doorbell rang right as I was coming back out, and Creed saved me from a dash across the apartment to get the door.

"That'll be Meredith," he said.

After a cursory glance through the peephole, he opened the door.

"Thank you for coming."

"Any time, really. I got Sofie and Danny dropped off at school, so it's no trouble. What happened?"

65

"Hellhound ambushed us as we were coming home. I think my arm is broken, but I'll take that over a broken neck any day."

Meredith smiled. "A broken arm, I can fix. A broken neck, not so much. Did it break from a fall?"

"No, it bit me."

The clinical focus in her gaze failed to hold back a momentary concern. A bite could be disastrous, considering we didn't know the potential effects.

"Let's have a look."

Creed's movements were stiff as he slid off his leather jacket. "I don't think the teeth punched through."

"You're right," Meredith agreed. Relief. "There's no blood. I'd hate for us to find out the hard way what their bite does."

She rubbed her palms together, summoning the divine healing ability. Placing her hands on Creed's arm, she closed her eyes and concentrated. A moment later, he was rotating it, testing the healed bone and declaring it good as new.

"Amazing. I would've been in a cast for weeks."

"Does it drain you very much?" I asked.

"Not a straightforward injury like that, not much. It takes more energy to get my two hellions ready for school," Meredith laughed.

"If they're anything like Dylan and I were as kids, I can only imagine. Can I get you some coffee?"

"I'd love some. I can't stay long, but tell me more about this hellhound. I'm worried about it being out during the day."

She and Creed settled onto barstools at the kitchen counter while I pulled out three mugs and filled them.

"I think it was more that I flushed it out from a hiding spot," Creed said.

The entire ordeal sent a new tingle down my spine. There

weren't a lot of families with children there at the apartment complex, but there were some. Kids had a way of poking around in places adults might not. If one had wandered off to explore before school…

"You okay, sugar?"

Creed's voice interrupted my dark imaginings, and I looked down to find my hands frozen on the coffeepot. I let go and went back to adding cream or sugar to our liking.

"Sorry, I was just thinking how glad I am it was us who found that thing."

Meredith nodded. "I agree. Do you think it was just coincidence, it being here where you live?"

"I'm not sure," I shrugged. "We don't know much about them yet. It's not the first time I killed something nearby, though, and we all know it won't be the last."

Though the vampires tended to hunt on the edges of town, they had occasionally strayed into more central parts, like where my apartment was. It was a simple enough explanation that the hellhound had been on the hunt and prowled too far.

"Has Hugo told you about what I discussed with him last night?" Creed asked her.

"He has."

"And you came anyway."

It wasn't a question. He sounded like he was confirming something to himself.

"I think you'll find that every one of us cares more about your actions, your loyalty, and how you treat people than your parentage."

Creed nodded. "So far, that's unanimous."

"Believe us when we show you we're not going to throw you away. We Amasai stick together as a team. As a family. And you're part of that."

Creed seemed stunned to hear the sentiment from someone other than my brother or me so bluntly laid on the table. "I don't know what to say."

"You don't have to say anything. But stop worrying about what we think and work out what knowing about your father means to you." Meredith gracefully slipped off her barstool. "Thanks for the coffee."

"Any time," I told her. "Thanks for coming so fast and for the chat." I gave her a pointed look.

She smiled her warm smile, then turned to Creed and offered a hug. I couldn't pinpoint if it was her caregiving nature or because she was a mom, but her hugs were among the best. Whatever it was, Creed left the conversation, and the embrace, relieved—I could see that much in the set of his shoulders and less furrowed brow.

"For what it's worth, I agree with her," I said as I shut and locked the door behind Meredith. "You're looking at this new revelation through the lens of what we all might think about it and it's causing you unnecessary worry. Yescha said Azazel poses no threat, so you can safely stop and consider what all this means to you... and only you."

Creed rubbed at the spot where his arm had been broken. "You're both right. I think I just needed to know where I stand. Now, I can focus on what to do with the information. Long term, I mean. I've spent so many years questioning what I am. Now I know and it only opened up more questions."

"Do you regret finding out?"

"No, not at all. It's a shock to the system, but it beats the hell out of not knowing."

I covered a yawn with the back of my hand. "Good. I wouldn't want to be the one who pushed you into something that made you unhappy."

"You didn't push... too hard." Creed smiled and took my face in his hands, kissed me. "Why don't you go on to bed and get some sleep. I've got some things to think through and I doubt I'll knock off anytime soon."

"I understand. I'm here if you need me."

"I know." He answered me, but his thoughts were already a thousand miles away.

We had reached an impasse. There was nothing else I could do except reassure him I wouldn't run for the hills because we had learned an inconvenient truth. A truth that was now his to do with as he would.

Chapter 8

I woke up, stretched from my fingertips to my toes, turned over to reach for Creed, and found... nothing. Just a cold, empty side of the bed.

I tried not to let it bother me. He had, after all, said he had some thoughts to work through and wasn't ready to sleep. But he had never not come to bed. Since he had started staying with me, even after nights when his guilt about the zombies had been overwhelming, he would eventually settle down and be there when I woke up.

The apartment was quiet; so quiet, I thought he had fallen asleep on the couch.

My bare feet whispered across the carpet as I left my bedroom and went down the hall, and the scent of coffee wafted in my direction. That had me picking up the pace and rounding into the living room to find... Creed, still fully dressed, sitting at the dining room table with a cup of coffee in his hands. He was looking out the wide sliding glass door, focused on nothing in particular.

My entrance had been silent, so I cleared my throat to get his attention and not startle him. When he looked in my direction, he smiled, but the expression didn't quite reach his eyes. Their dark depths were veiled, haunted by thoughts I didn't understand.

All the same, I smiled back, trying to offer a sense of normalcy. An invitation to share his burden.

He started to rise from his seat. "Did you want some coffee?"

"Yes, but don't get up." I waved him off. "I'll get it and join you."

I poured myself a cup of joe, creamed and sugared it how I liked, and settled into the chair next to Creed. "Did you sleep today at all?"

"No. I tried, but never could settle myself."

"Do you wanna talk about it?"

Creed breathed a heavy sigh. "Honestly? Not really. I don't have anything to say that hasn't already been said, and I don't want to wear you out by beating a dead horse."

"But you won't—"

"You don't have to keep saying that. I know you want to help, but there's nothing you can do. Don't you understand this darkness inside me is dangerous? I see that now. You should, too." He paused and scrubbed his hands through his hair. "I'm sorry... Look, I have to get to work downtown, so I'm gonna head out. I just didn't wanna leave before you got up."

Sliding his chair out, he nearly knocked it over backward in his haste to escape. I got up, too, but he was already halfway out the door before I could react.

"Wait," I told him. "I thought you were on the graveyard shift?"

"I am, but... I... I need to go. See you in the morning."

He shut the door and was gone before I could say anything else. My eyes shifted to the clock on the wall that read 3:30 p.m. The night shift at the downtown pawnshop didn't start until eight o'clock, and that was only if the swing shift needed extra help. I frowned and sat back down to finish my coffee, guessing at what had made Creed so jumpy that he couldn't stand to be in my presence. He obviously had a lot to work through, so I tried not to take his rush to get away personally, but thought maybe I had been crowding him in my drive to find the truth.

The truth was supposed to set you free. I wasn't so sure in this case.

Sunset was coming in less than two hours, so I decided not to stew and go get myself ready to be on watch that night. I had wanted to get in early and let the others know about the silver bullets working for killing the hellhounds as Garret had suggested, but now I needed to get my mind off Creed and how he had left.

Seeing Solomon's car parked in the driveway in front of our farmhouse headquarters was a welcome surprise. I didn't care what he was there to tell us or discuss with us; a visit from the detective was a break from the usual.

"Remi. Just the woman I was looking for," he said when I came through the front door.

Hugo, Aric, and Garret were standing in the center of our gathering area with Solomon, and their conversation ceased when Sol greeted me.

I allowed a thin laugh. "Good or bad?"

"Good… Or, as good as it can be," he answered. "I have news about the Triple Six trial. Do you want to talk privately?"

"No, that's okay. Everyone else here is just as invested in it as I am."

"My thoughts exactly. And if things move quickly enough, they may find out in the newspaper, anyway," Solomon said. "The Creek County DA might be close to reaching a plea deal. Some high-powered trial lawyer out of Dallas came to assist, pro bono. Found some new strings to pull to get their attorneys to the table. Nice lady."

I could see from the way he said it, she had used his well-collected evidence to move things along rather than shouldering a small-town detective out of her way.

"Say, isn't your brother a lawyer in Dallas?" he asked.

"Yeah, he's in corporate law, but something tells me he had a hand in this. So, what happens if they reach a deal?"

"It's life without parole for all of them, which is better than the capital punishment they could receive if convicted and sentenced by a jury... Better for them, that is. But you or your brother won't have to testify and there won't be a change of venue due to the circumstances."

"Sounds all very neat and tidy," I commented.

After saying it aloud, I thought it really did feel like James was behind it. He would want our father's killers to all go away with minimal fuss and without a court circus, which was what was bound to happen if too much truth came out on the witness stand. But if there was the guarantee of them all ending up in the slammer for life, I didn't blame him for engineering the outcome.

"It should be... Which is what you want, right?"

I nodded. "That's exactly what I want. Dylan, too. I'll call him after I hit the road."

"This is great news, *mija*," Hugo said. "It will be good to have it behind you."

"It's not done yet... But you're right. Just having those people locked away where they can't be out in the world again hurting people will be a welcome relief. Even if I did still want a piece of them."

"I needed to talk to Jocelyn, too," Sol said. "Is she around tonight?"

"No, she's working the swing shift today. Won't be in," Aric answered.

"Wish I could say it was more good news, but… Well, it's not my place to share, so I'll say no more. Which shop will she be working in?"

"Downtown Westview. She'll be there for another few hours," I said.

It hadn't occurred to me before, but she and Creed would overlap by a couple of hours. That is, if he had gone straight to work as he said.

The detective glanced at his watch. "I don't have any more calls tonight, so that works out well. Oh, and Remi, thanks again for the heads up about the hellhound situation this morning. We did get a few calls, but were able to reassure folks that everything was fine. It's far easier with you all being out in the open."

"It has been easier for us, too," Hugo said. "So far."

"I'll get out of here. I know it's time for y'all to get ready to head out," Sol said.

"Thank you for coming to tell me about the trial," I said.

He waved a hand on his way out the door. "Any time."

As he was going out, Gabriel was coming in. They paused long enough to clap palms in a friendly handshake and exchange quick greetings.

"Why was Sol here?" Gabe asked when he joined us.

"Let's head to the armory," I said. "We'll fill you in on the way."

Since it was closing in on the time when we would need to get out into the field for the night, we could talk while we got ready. I told him about the possible plea bargain for the Triple Six as we crossed the yard in the fading light.

"In terms of simplicity, that's the best potential outcome," my partner said. "It'll save you and Dylan a trip to the witness stand, and the whole story won't have to be trotted out again."

He wasn't wrong. I hadn't had a chance to mull it over, but the small, vindictive part of me that had been hoping for a death sentence across the board was shrinking in favor of reason. A life behind bars was no life at all.

Hugo entered the code and unlocked things as we talked, the conversation moving seamlessly to the hellhound incident that morning.

"I wanted to tell you that the silver bullets work," I said, heading for the section of weapons that belonged to me.

"Who had to shoot one last night?" Gabe asked.

I strapped a trio of stakes into my left boot. "Actually, I shot one this morning outside my apartment building."

My partner glanced toward our leader and I interrupted before he could ask. "Hugo already knows. Meredith had to come fix Creed's arm afterward. I'll tell you all about it later, but suffice to say they're brazen enough to come into town where there are more people. And, the silver bullet idea was a good one on Garret's part."

"Let's go check out the area tonight, see if we can figure out what lured it there. Did you get any details about where it was hiding?" Gabriel asked as he added a few bolts to his quiver.

"No, I didn't look too closely. There were a few people watching, and Creed was hurt so we went straight inside after I killed it."

"That's okay, we'll go do that now. Hugo, if it's good with you, Remi and I will take town tonight?"

"Good. Aric and I will cover ground near the lake, where the two of you killed those other hounds night before last."

I pulled my jacket on over the holsters for knives that I wore and double checked my weaponry. Stakes, throwing knives, silver daggers, holy water, extra mags… My handgun never left the small of my back, so once I zipped up my jacket, I was fully strapped with the addition of my bow and quiver.

"I'm ready when y'all are," I announced.

"Slow poke," Aric said, crunching a peanut M&M between his teeth. "Too much talking going on—I was ready ten minutes ago."

"Keep talking like that and I'll hide all the Dr. Peppers," I warned.

He feigned horror. "You monster. You wouldn't."

"Try me," I grinned.

It was a welcome change of pace to leave the armory with some levity, even under the shadow of uncertainty we experienced each night. We parted ways at the end of the driveway: Gabe and I going left into Dove Creek, Hugo and Aric to the right toward the lake.

"I just need to call Dylan real quick, while we're on the way in. I told Sol I'd let him know about our dad's trial."

"Sure thing," Gabe said. "I'm just gonna go park at Bobby Sue's like we usually do, so we can cover some ground on foot tonight."

"Perfect. I'll just be a minute."

I pulled out my phone and hit my brother's name in the recent contacts. He answered after only a couple rings, and I told him what the detective had asked me to relay. His relief was palpable enough to travel over a wireless connection, the momentary silence heavy in the air.

"Dyl? You still with me?"

"Huh? Yeah, yeah… still here. I was just thinking about how I didn't wanna testify, and now I won't have to if it works out."

The ordeal had been horrific for all of us involved, but Dylan had had the added torment of not only coming to find our father's lifeless body in my grip but to have witnessed Diana's murder and been taken hostage by Cerise's sycophants. It didn't strain logic to understand why he wouldn't want to relive that night.

"One other thing, then I have to go... Solomon was on his way to see Joss. He said he didn't want to tell us about it since it wasn't his news to tell, but it didn't sound good."

"Wonder what it is?"

"No doubt you'll find out soon enough. But I wanted you to know in case she needs a shoulder."

"Thanks, Rem. Y'all be safe tonight."

"Always. Talk to you later."

Gabe swung his car into the narrow parking lot of Bobby Sue's Diner and chose an empty spot that faced the sidewalk. "Do you think Joss is okay? I can't imagine she's in some kind of trouble."

"No, I don't think it was that," I said as I popped the latch on my seatbelt. "It didn't sound terrible or urgent, but Sol said it wasn't good news."

"Then I guess we'll find out if she wants us to."

The diner didn't get a big dinner rush on Mondays, so there was no one around when we got out and got our bows and quivers into place. It was getting dark so early, people didn't seem to be out as much. But the coming Friday marked the beginning of the holiday shopping season, which meant that would soon change.

The small apartment complex I lived in was about three blocks in front of us, the two-story buildings just visible above the rooflines of the houses in between. We started walking, and

I recalled what had happened the last time my partner and I had come this way. I was certain I would never be able to erase the image of him bleeding and unconscious on the pavement while Valan threatened me.

My steps stuttered for a few paces before I fell back into rhythm.

"All right there?" Gabe asked.

"Yup. Fine and dandy." He gave me the side-eye, and I shrugged in return. "What?"

"For one, you just said 'fine and dandy.' And second, you're obviously not."

"My brain's just all over the place right now," I admitted. "The Triple Six trial... Creed... this hellhound thing. I guess I'm jumpy. And then I thought about when you and I came this way a few months ago."

"Let's take a minute, then," he said, pausing on the sidewalk. "I don't want you to get hurt because you're distracted."

"I can usually tune it all out..."

"I know you can. Let's talk through the hellhound attack this morning. Maybe that will help you get your thoughts in order. Unless there's something else you want to talk about?"

"No, that's good. That's what I need to focus on, anyway," I said.

I took him through the order of how things happened, how we noticed the smell of the thing and flushed it out rather than it coming after us, how I incinerated it with the Holy Light, Creed's broken arm... Every detail I could recall.

"Do you know exactly where it was hiding before it attacked Creed?"

"Not exactly since I was so far away, but there's only one place it could've been."

"Let's go check it out, if you're ready."

"I'm ready."

We resumed our short trek, and while my thoughts were still weighty, I didn't feel as scattered as when we set out. And Gabriel was right: Distraction could lead to disaster if we ran into trouble.

We had to cross the parking lot to get to my building, where my Jeep was parked but Creed's Escalade was not. Like I had expected him to come back when he ran out on me as fast as a chicken with a fox in the coop?

I led the way around the side of the building where we had killed the hellhound. There was an alcove under the stairs and between the entries to the lower level apartments where our mailboxes were located, which was the hidey-hole I assumed the beast had used. Gabe pulled out his phone and turned on the flashlight to see better and poke around inside it.

"I wonder if they're susceptible to sunlight like their vampire owners," he said.

"I'm not sure. From this angle, we were never in direct sunlight since it was so early, but this faces north and isn't in full sun at all this time of year. It might have chosen its spot well."

He muttered something to himself that sounded like 'inconclusive,' while taking his mental notes, and I couldn't have agreed more. There was a lot of inconclusive going around.

Shining his light in all the corners, he came to an abrupt stop. He plucked something from under the small bank of mailboxes and studied it for a moment.

"Rem, come here. You need to see this."

Chapter 9

I left my post outside the alcove, watching for intruders of either the human or vampire variety, and turned to Gabriel to look at what he had found. He held up an arrow.

Not just any arrow—one of mine. No one else would carry silver broadheads with wooden shafts.

"That could have come from anywhere," I said. "I do live right upstairs."

"Look closer. It's bloody. Two of the wings on the head are bent."

So it was an arrow I had shot and it had hit my target. That much was obvious. But what had been my target? If the hellhound had carried the arrow here...

"It's from the vampire I hit in the gut the other night, isn't it?"

"I think he sent this hound after you in retaliation. It might be time to rethink our strategy. If every time we leave a vamp wounded, it comes after one of us, it's not worth the risk."

I nodded in agreement. That hadn't been a factor when we were discussing the plan not to eject the demons from their hosts. Still, I wasn't sure it was worth throwing out the entire playbook because I had called the wrong play.

"What if we leave nothing behind? Leave nothing to track. This was an early misstep."

One I could chalk up to being distracted by what the bloodsucker had been wheezing on about. I had been more focused on the information our interrogation had divulged than on cleaning up after ourselves. But to be fair to myself, my partner hadn't thought about the arrow, either.

"You have a point," Gabe said, coming out of the alcove and back onto the sidewalk.

He stuck the arrow in his own quiver, where it stood out like a giant among men. I guessed that was the idea—in mine, it was identical to all the others and I might pull it by mistake.

Squatting down, he took his light and studied the smudge of blood the hellbeast had left on the edge of the sidewalk and in the dormant yellow grass. It was a red so dark it was nearly black, and looked oily and sludgy. The kind of stain that would take a good pressure wash from the maintenance crew to be cleaned off, and even then I wasn't sure that would get rid of it.

"You said the body incinerated when you hit it with your light?"

"Yeah, it completely withered away."

Gabe righted himself and switched off the light, put his phone back in his pocket.

"Next time we come across a hellhound, can you try killing it with just the light?"

"You bet. With a gun in my other hand."

He chuckled. "Better safe than sorry."

"Do you wanna walk for a little while, see if there are any other hounds that found a place to hole up for the day?"

"Yes, definitely. If you're good for that?"

"My lid's screwed on straight now. Promise."

As long as I didn't think too closely about the possibility of an encore performance from Valan.

The thing was, though, in gaining more control over the Holy Light, I felt less afraid. My only hang-up was if the ancient vampire got the drop on my partner again. I knew I could handle a threat to myself alone.

We made a strategic loop through the apartment complex, eyeballing all the alcoves and other areas that would have provided protection from the sun during the day. Though we didn't know for certain the hellhounds had to avoid the rays, it was a likely assumption.

Once we all-cleared the quartet of buildings, we moved on to the neighborhood that lay between the rentals and the city center. Christmas lights were already showing up in the rows of neat little houses, but for every eave and fence that sported the twinklers, another porch still held pumpkins and little hay bales as though the owners were resolute in hanging on to fall until they had had their fill of turkey.

"So how is Creed doing after everything that's happened?"

I hesitated, a noncommittal sound coming from the back of my throat. "It's…" *It sucks. He suddenly doesn't want to be around me. I think I overstepped.* "Complicated."

Gabe glanced at me. "I'm sorry, I didn't mean to pry. When I asked earlier what was bothering you, Creed was on your list."

"No need to apologize. You're not prying. But I feel like I'm always unloading my baggage right onto your doorstep, and that's not fair to you."

"I wouldn't ask if I didn't want to help. Besides, I vent to you, too, when I need to. I know your ear is always available," Gabe said.

We reached the row of identical buildings that held all the entities relevant to running our small town: post office, city office, activity center, among others. They were all dim for the night, only street lamps and security lights inside on at the increasingly late hour. I paused in front of the city office, under one of the steel awnings that overhung the sidewalk.

"And it is, but you don't have many occasions to exercise that tit for tat. You have to admit, I have far more problems to bend your ear about than you do mine," I insisted.

"That may be the reality of your situation now, but there may come a time when it's me who's in need more."

"Doubt it," I muttered. "You always have your crap together."

His lips turned up ever so slightly. "Mostly," he agreed. "I stayed after you for a long time to open up to me—I'm not afraid of what's there and I asked for it. So don't feel like you're some kind of burden to me, because you're not."

I shook my head and blinked hard a few times. "I don't deserve you. Not after the way I treated you for so long."

"Let's not go there. I wasn't always the easiest to get along with, so let's not dredge up past sins." He put an arm around my shoulders and gave me a squeeze. "Come on... Miss Ginger's is open for a few more minutes. Let's hurry and get some coffees to go since it's getting cold out here."

* * *

The next couple days sailed by without us seeing any more sign of hellhounds, but we wound a couple vamps to the point of being incapable of harming the humans they were hunting. It remained to be seen whether they, too, would seek revenge for their injuries, so we all stayed on our guard in case of any more demon dogs lying in wait.

There was still an uncrossable chasm that lay between Creed and me, but he was at least being polite about it. As in, not running from the room when I tried to talk to him. But I gave him his space. I knew what it was to want time and room to breathe, think, and process.

When Thursday came around, I wondered if he was still up to coming with me to celebrate Thanksgiving with my family. There were no excuses to be had—all three pawnshops were closed that day and night, and while we were all technically on call, the Amasai were taking it easy on rotation that night. Considering demons didn't observe man-made holidays, there was still a good chance some of us would see action, despite it being a time of giving thanks. But there was no solid reason for Creed to break his commitment to going unless he flat didn't want to go.

I pulled two coffee mugs out of the cupboard and filled mine as far as I could with room for creamer. About the time I finished stirring, Creed came into the kitchen, still sleepy-eyed and groggy. With his tousled wavy hair, it was usually one of my favorite looks on him, but not so in that moment. Though he had made every effort to rest and I had even heard him breathing the deep, even rhythm of sleep, the dark circles under his eyes told on his inability to settle down. His grogginess was from this lack of respite rather than a result of us pulling an all morning sheet-tangling lovemaking session.

And that hit me right in the gut.

"Hey there. Coffee?" I asked.

"Hey, sugar. Yes, please," he murmured.

I poured coffee into the other mug I had pulled down, added just a hint of sugar and left it black how he liked it. He joined me at the counter and gave me a gentle kiss on the side of my neck.

"Sorry I slept so late," he said. "We're not gonna be late to your mom's, are we?"

I lifted one shoulder in a half-shrug and handed him the coffee. "Don't worry about it—I just got up not long ago myself. We have a couple hours still, so plenty of time."

I wanted to ask him how he had slept, what plan of action he had settled on, but didn't risk frightening away any and all conversation by delving deeper than pleasantries. What the hell, I was happy just knowing he still intended to join us for Thanksgiving dinner. That was a start.

"Are we taking anything that we need to prepare?" Creed asked.

"No, I picked up rolls from Miss Ginger's yesterday, so we're all set," I told him. "I would offer to make us something to eat, but I planned on saving room, if you know what I mean."

He smiled. Not one of his dazzlers, but for a moment the clouds cleared and the sun shone.

"I know exactly what you mean. Solid strategy."

I didn't have long to linger, since actually washing, drying, and fixing my hair would take time, and I didn't want to be late. But when the silence stretched out between us—me uncertain of what I should and shouldn't bring up, Creed with more on his mind than was good for him—I used getting ready as an excuse to bug out even sooner than I had intended.

"Listen, I wanted to get dressed up for the occasion, so I'm gonna go get started," I told him. "But if you need anything..."

"I know where to find you," he finished with another small smile.

It took every bit as long as I thought it would to get my hair into nicely styled waves, complete with the appropriate products and even hairspray. Still, by the time I finished with it, my make-up, and got my clothes together, I was pleased to have put in the effort. In a dark red blouse with black wool trousers and nice high heels, I didn't look ready to hunt demons and hellhounds like I normally did.

Nevermind that the higher rise waistband of the pants was the perfect place to stash my handgun.

Or that the crucifix I always wore hung beautifully with the neckline of the blouse.

Creed was dapper in his dark rinse jeans and a black sweater, his springtime mountain scent extra tempting to my senses since he was fresh from the shower. His gaze lingered on me with an appreciation I was glad to see hadn't evaporated with his mental burdens.

"You look beautiful," he told me.

"Thank you. You clean up pretty well yourself."

We kept the conversation light on the way to Westview, only discussing how the entire SUV smelled of perfectly baked bread courtesy of Miss Ginger's, how nice the landscape looked bathed in autumn oranges and yellows, and how Creed was looking forward to finally meeting my mom and her husband, Hadden.

Neither Jocelyn's car nor Dylan's truck were outside when we arrived at my mom's house, so we were the first to get there. Creed parked his Escalade in the driveway and came around to open my door for me and help with the pink and white striped bakery box.

My mom greeted us at the front door, the inviting aroma of home cooking wafting out as she waved us inside.

"Come on in... I'm so glad to see both of you!"

"Hi, Mom. Happy Thanksgiving."

She wrapped me in a tight embrace and commented on how she liked the red blouse I wore before turning to Creed and offering her hand.

"You must be Creed. Welcome."

"Yes, ma'am," he said, accepting her hand with both of his own. "Pleased to meet you."

"Likewise," she smiled. "Looking forward to getting to know you better."

When Creed looked at me like a deer in headlights, she rescued him from his momentary panic.

"Don't worry, hon. Remi has already told me all about your background and you won't find any judgement here."

"Uh," Creed stuttered, like he wasn't quite sure what to say. "Thank you. I'm glad there's honesty between us and we won't have to sidestep it."

My petite mother smiled up at him and patted his hand. "Both of you come in and make yourselves comfortable. Hadden is just finishing up in the kitchen, and Jocelyn and Dylan should be here any moment."

We didn't have to wait long for my brother and Joss, which I was grateful for if for no other reason than to save Creed from feeling the need to crawl under the table and hide.

They joined us in the living room, hugs and cheerful chatter filling the space. Hadden came out from the kitchen to announce dinner was ready, pleased that he had it all cooked and organized on time.

My mom had decorated and table-scaped the dining room in an elegant fall theme with candles here and there along with her best place settings. She seemed proud to show off her knack for setting the scene, and Jocelyn praised her good taste.

We all took our places around the table; Mom and Hadden at the two ends, Creed and I facing Joss and Dylan on each side. There was pleasant small talk as we passed around side dishes of herbed mashed potatoes and cornbread stuffing, among other things—many, many other things. Hadden carved the turkey and made sure everyone got the exact slices they wanted.

"I know," he said when we were all finished filling our plates. "Let's go around the table and say what we're thankful for." When we all giggled, he smiled. "It's cheesy, I know, but it's important we celebrate the real reason for the holiday. I'll start—I'm giving thanks for this house and everyone in it today, the ability to put together a splendid meal, and most of all... my brilliant and beautiful wife."

My mom beamed at him across the table, but it was Dylan who looked like he was about to burst. He allowed our mom her moment to bask in her husband's praise, then spoke up.

"Me next." He grinned and turned to Jocelyn. "It's you I'm thankful for, and I want to give thanks for you every day, for the rest of my life."

He left his chair and got down on one knee, producing a glimmering diamond ring from his shirt pocket. Joss gasped before he popped the question, the tears in her eyes rivaling the sparkle of the ring. The rest of us held our breath in rapt anticipation.

"Jocelyn Marie Benton, will you do me the most incredible honor of becoming my wife?"

"Yes! Oh my goodness, yes."

They both got to their feet, and he slid the ring onto her finger before they hugged each other and shared a sweet kiss. Joss brushed tears from her cheeks before she sat back down and tried to catch her breath.

"Well, that was just beautiful," our mom said, tears in her own eyes. "And a most welcome surprise."

"I was afraid to say anything," Dylan said. "I kept the whole thing to myself so I wouldn't slip up and give away the secret."

I smiled. "That was a wise plan."

We didn't keep up with the round-robin of what we were all thankful for—anything after Dylan's proposal would pale in comparison. But I had plenty of things I would give thanks for, even in the midst of the turmoil with Creed. Not the least of which was gaining a sister.

Chapter 10

I stood at the sink with my mom, drying dishes with a kitchen towel as she washed and handed them to me. It seemed a mundane task after the excitement at dinner, but the dishwasher couldn't hold everything after such a decadent meal.

The others were outside, sitting around a fire in the firepit, leaving us to have a moment of quiet. In the months of tumult that started back in the summer, my mom and I hadn't had a proper chat. It made the time to ourselves welcome.

"Creed seems like a nice young man," she said as she handed me a dripping plate.

I nodded. "He is. I really like him."

"But?"

How on earth she knew there was a 'but' without me saying anything was a mystery to me. Probably one I wouldn't solve until I became a mother myself. *If…*

"But I feel like I'm losing him," I confessed.

A metric ton came off my shoulders when I said it aloud. To anyone else, I would have felt like I was admitting defeat. But if anyone else could truly understand where I was, it was her.

"You mean since you learned about his father?"

She handed me a glass—crystal for the occasion rather than

the everyday jelly jars, so I was careful as I dried it.

"Yes. Ever since we saw Yescha, there's something between us. Some weird gap I can't bridge." I set down the glass and looked at the running tap. "It's like trying to catch water with only my hands, trying to get back what we had."

"Your relationship may never be the same," she said.

I blinked. Totally not what I thought she'd say. But I was glad for the lack of empty platitudes and for cutting straight to the truth.

She passed another plate into my hands. "People change. Circumstances change. Decide if the change is something you work through or if it's a deal-breaker."

With the dripping wet plate in my hands, I considered whether Creed's dark heritage was something that mattered enough to me to end our union. After all, I had point blank told two angels I wouldn't leave him—had it been the buzz of finding out that had been talking, or was I truly ready to stand by him for the long haul?

Did it matter to him? Was that why he was holding me at arm's length?

"Pick up the pace, Remi-Jean," my mom snapped me out of it with the gentle command.

I finished drying the plate and took the serving bowl from her.

"He's convinced the darkness in him is dangerous," I said quietly.

"With what you all see every night, it's easy to think of darkness and light as opposing forces. But they're not mutually exclusive. We all have our dark parts and our light. It's what we do with those that matters. It's the side we let win that defines us."

It was simple, but significant. And she was completely right.

I took a deep breath. "I forget you lived it with Dad for so long."

Rinsing a handful of silverware, she said, "John was a good man until the bitter end. But he went through a spell where he lost his faith, and I couldn't help him."

That was a revelation to me. "So it wasn't the drinking?"

"That was the pain point, without a doubt, but it was the cause of the drinking and us as a family no longer being enough that ended John and me."

"We haven't really talked about it like this before," I commented.

"Well, for a while, you were too young to discuss it in any detail. Then, you and Dominic got serious, and no one wants to rain on new love by reopening old wounds. And the last few years have brought you enough hurts without rehashing old ones," my mom said.

Tears flooded my eyes at the thought of my late husband. "I miss him... I still miss him."

Mom dried her hands and reached up to stroke my hair. "I know, baby girl. You always will, but it gets easier."

"What can I do to help Creed?" I took a breath and refocused on the trouble in front of me.

"Be present," she said. "Ultimately, it's his decision and his alone to be what he wants to be. But as long as you're on the same team and pulling in the same direction, you can make it work."

She held out her arms and I hugged her. I had been a daddy's girl growing up, always seeking him out first when I had even the pettiest of grievances to sort through. But in the intervening years since he had not only split with Mom but moved away from the rest of us, it was her I had come to rely on. I was fortunate to have her steady presence.

The patio door slid open, and we heard Jocelyn as she came into the kitchen.

"It's really nice outside, but the men started talking about fishing... Oh, am I interrupting?"

I smiled. "No, not at all."

Mom smiled at Joss, too. "I'm afraid I'm not much of a fishing enthusiast, so Hadden doesn't get much from talking to me about it. He'll be bending their ear for a while."

"That's okay," Joss giggled. "I'm not into fishing, either, so I thought I'd come in and see if I can help."

The sink was empty, and she had helped us package the leftovers and clear the table earlier, so there was nothing left to be done that I could see.

"You know what you girls can help me with?" my mom asked. She took the pumpkin pie from the counter. "There's not enough of this left to fuss with keeping it. Let's finish it off."

I grinned. "I'm game."

"I'll get plates," Jocelyn offered.

"Don't bother," Mom said, grabbing three forks.

We sat at the kitchen table, devouring the last of the dessert straight from the pie tin.

"I think you better show us that ring again," my mom said.

Joss' radiant smile was ear-to-ear when she held out her left hand for us to inspect. The sparkler glinted under the lights, and it reminded me of how she had envied mine. Not the ring itself, but what it symbolized.

Oh, how the roles had reversed. Joss was just starting that journey with Dylan, and I was left to wonder what the future held for Creed and me. But she and my brother deserved every bit of happiness they had with each other, so I would gladly take on the uncertainty I was enduring rather than trade places with them.

"Remi, do you want to do some shopping tomorrow?" Joss asked. Before I could decline because of my natural aversion to retail therapy, she sweetened the invitation. "It'll be anti-Black Friday shopping, at the small shops there at Creek Crossing. I could use a little girl time."

The last sentence was full of an implied plea for some alone time to have a conversation, so I didn't make her ask another way.

"Sure, that would be fun. I was afraid you wanted to go to the mall here in Westview."

"No, it's to be avoided like the plague tomorrow. Even I wouldn't set foot in there."

"It might be early to ask, but where will you go dress shopping?" my mom asked.

"Oh no, definitely not too early—I've had this all planned since I was young, and I didn't get to have the perfect wedding the first time around. Mockingbird Lane in Dallas is where all the best dress shops are. I'd love for you both to come with me when I schedule it."

"Of course I'll be there. I'm honored for you to include me," Mom said.

"Me, too. I know it's not my thing, but this is huge. Dress shopping will be second only to the Big Day."

Joss nodded with enough vigor to set her beautiful curls bouncing. "I know, right?"

My mom raised her eyebrows at me. "You're one to talk, Remi-Jean. You tried on two dresses. Only *two*. And you chose the first one."

"When you know, you know."

She polished off the last bite of pumpkin pie. "To be fair, it was a gorgeous dress. Only someone as tall as you could have made it work like you did."

Jocelyn held up her hands. "Okay, now I *have* to see this dress."

"I have the photo album from the wedding... If it's okay with you?" my mom asked me.

"I'm sorry, I didn't think," Joss said. "We don't have to—"

"No, please. It's perfectly fine. I don't mind."

The truth was that I enjoyed reminiscing about the good times, holding on to the precious memories that were all I had left of that happy time in my life.

Mom went and fetched the album from a shelf in the living room where she kept all her photo books. She came back toting the thick, faux-leather binder that held hundreds of pictures and laid it out on the kitchen table between us. The very first page was a full-page photo of me in my wedding dress. It was a smaller twin to the huge, matted and framed photograph my mom kept hanging in the long hallway that led to the bedrooms.

I was only twenty-two... fresh-faced and young, full of hope as I stood under a weeping willow on the venue's extensive grounds. I could still remember the feeling of the white satin against my skin, the scent of the roses and lily-of-the-valley tied into a pretty bouquet in my hands, the warm June afternoon barely two weeks after I had graduated college.

Three short years later, I was robbed of that doe-eyed, newlywed hope. Of those dreams for a long life with Dominic.

But the bitterness of loss didn't settle in like it had done in the intervening years. Instead, another brick in the wall of my resolve snapped into place. I was no longer floundering, drowning in a sea of sadness and revenge.

I smiled a slow smile.

As if they had been waiting for my reaction to delving into the past, my mom and Joss resumed their happy chatter.

"That really was some dress," Jocelyn said. "Do you have a picture of the back?"

"Oh, there's a perfect one during the ceremony. Let me find it..."

My mom flipped a few pages back and found a shot the photographer had taken from behind me, focused on Dom at the exact moment he was putting the ring on my finger. While the others looked at the style of my dress, I looked at the expression on his face. The way he looked at me, like he had won both the lottery and a one-way ticket to heaven.

Creed didn't look at me that way. There was certainly affection and appreciation in the way he gazed at me, but it was dim in comparison to how my husband had looked at me.

Joss and my mom continued to rave about the venue—the Museum of Fine Arts there in Westview—the bridesmaids' dresses, the flowers...

* * *

"Did you have fun talking about wedding stuff with your mom and Joss?" Creed asked.

We were on our way home, the evening a pleasant one even though rain threatened. The interior of the car smelled of homemade dishes like mashed potatoes and roasted vegetables, turkey and dressing, the leftovers from Thanksgiving dinner carefully packed by Mom and Hadden.

"I did, actually. I thought I would hate talking about somebody else's wedding when the time came, but it turns out, it's not a bad thing."

Creed glanced at me from the side, then smiled. "I'm glad it wasn't a painful conversation for you."

The thing was, wedding talk could grow awkward between a couple who weren't on the same page, and I was pretty sure Creed and I weren't even reading from the same novel. I changed the subject before I somehow mistakenly gave the impression that I was trying to wrangle him into a trip down the aisle.

"Sorry you got leashed into entertaining Hadden's fishing obsession earlier. I hope you weren't bored," I said.

"No, not at all. I haven't gone in a long time, but I love fishing. He even told us about some of his best spots around here. It was nice to talk about something mundane for a change."

It was like somebody switched on the light. "That's why you've been so distant lately, isn't it? You want to avoid the conversations about you and what you are."

"Not exactly. It's not you... Not really. We talk about anything and everything, but everybody else has wanted to show solidarity or whatever it is you'd call it. We don't have normal conversations anymore."

"It hasn't been that long—barely a week. And isn't it a good thing that they want to show you they're with you, even after everything that has happened?"

Creed parked in the spot next to my truck and cut the engine. He shifted in the driver's seat to face me. "Yes, and you have no idea what that means to me. But I know I'm also now the weak link on the team. A liability."

"No, you're—" I tried to interrupt him and tell him that wasn't true, but he didn't let me.

"It's true. I'm part of the same group of monsters we hunt

97

every night."

"To be part of it would mean you take part in what they do, which you don't. You aren't some label the supernatural world puts on you. You are what you choose to be."

I unlatched my seatbelt and got out of the SUV. Creed followed suit from the other side and met me on the sidewalk.

"You're annoyed with me," he said.

"No, not at all. But if I'm honest, I don't understand why you think your bloodline determines who you are. So you're Nephilim, the son of a Fallen... Why does that mean you have to repeat your father's mistakes?"

"It doesn't, but don't you think we all have a destiny? That our fates are predetermined? You yourself are an example. Your father was a hunter, now look at you. Look at Dylan."

"Yeah, my dad was a hunter, but I was also all set up to be a museum administrator before Dominic was killed. So what? We all have the free will to become what we choose to be."

"Do we, though? Your path was so altered by your husband's death, what else could it be but fate?"

I ground my molars as my frustration ignited. "It. Was. My. Choice. It was an ancient evil and an old vendetta that got Dom killed, and I chose to do something about it. I could've gone on with my plans alone, but didn't want to. If I have the ability to stop the same thing that happened to me from happening to other people, but do nothing about it, what does that make me? So no... It's not fate or destiny or any other hokey horse shit. I choose to fight."

"Point taken," Creed grinned.

Looking at him with disbelief, I questioned, "Then why are you smiling?"

"You make me enjoy being wrong."

I exhaled all at once and laughed a sharp laugh. It was easy to appreciate someone who would admit they were wrong, even if he was the one who had gotten me all riled up in the first place. And I felt the vise grip around my heart release at the sight of his high-wattage smile.

His eyes dropped to my lips. "Are you gonna hit me if I kiss you right now?"

"Not this time," I smiled.

Chapter 11

Creed was still in bed when I awoke, but he was sitting up and wide awake as though he had been for hours. Maybe even hadn't gone to sleep at all.

My content smile faded, erased by the unease that had returned to him.

"What is it? What's wrong?" I asked, sitting up and bringing the sheet with me.

A few moments of silence dragged on, and he didn't look at me. About the time I thought he had gone catatonic, he answered.

"I know what I have to do, and you aren't going to like it."

I sat up even straighter and braced myself for what was coming. "Tell me."

"I need to find my father. I need to find others like me, to figure out what I am. And I can't stay here to do that," he said.

"I don't understand," I told him. "Now we know what you are. And you're the same person, regardless of what label is put on your parentage."

"Except I'm not. I can feel it. Something inside me has changed in knowing, and none of you look at me the same way. Like you all can sense it even though you've tried not to let it color your opinion of me. It's like I'm a bomb you're all waiting to go off. And you know what? You're right. Look at what happened last time I put my faith in the wrong place."

I reached out and took his hands in mine. "You made a mistake, but you fixed it. Nothing like the cemetery will happen again."

"How do you know that? I harness the souls of the dead, Remi. There's nothing good about that. Never has been, and I've known that as long as I've known about my ability. No matter how hard I've tried to use it for good, it gets twisted back into what it truly is."

"So you're giving up?"

"No, but I need to know more. I need to know if it's even possible to be what I want to be. I have no idea how other Nephilim live, *if* they live at all. What are their abilities, how do they use them? I feel like I'm in the dark even more than I was before."

I nodded. "I understand that... I won't stop you from doing what you feel is right."

"Come with me," he said.

Letting go of his hands, I didn't know what to say. I didn't want him to continue to flounder here if he felt like the answers were elsewhere in the world, but I had too much to lose if I left Dove Creek to follow him.

You have to decide if the change is something you work through or if it's a deal-breaker.

"I can't," I said at last. "You know I can't."

"Can't or won't?"

I thought about that question for a moment, and found the truthful answer. "Both. There's too much work left to do. I refuse to leave that behind and break promises to the others. They need me... and I need them. As long as the Amasai are together, I'm part of that."

"Will you wait for me?"

We had barely survived the distance of the past week while we were under the same roof. I doubted the rift between us would close if it became physical, too.

"I promise to try. But I can't wait forever."

"If circumstances were different… If it was just you and me, none of this other stuff… Would you come with me?"

"I don't know… maybe? Probably."

Creed placed a solemn kiss on my lips. "I'll miss you."

I nodded. "I'll miss you, too. When do you plan to go?"

"Honestly, there's no point in dragging it out. I'll be out today."

I thought of Jocelyn and the plans we had made to get together later in the day. Though I didn't feel up to shopping, the idea of getting out of the apartment while Creed gathered his things felt better than sitting around in a miserable situation.

"I'm supposed to meet Joss later. I'll get out of your way so you can do what you need to do."

And didn't that statement have meaning on so many levels.

I would keep my chin up and get out of his way without clinging to what might have been, in a desperate bid to hold us together.

Getting out of the bed to go get ready, I took a pointer from something Creed had said: No point in dragging it out.

I texted Joss to ask if she wanted to meet a little earlier than planned. Nine times out of ten, I would have gone to Gabriel to hash out a problem, but this wasn't ordinary. For all his intentions to be a shoulder for me to cry on when I needed it, I didn't think he could quite understand where I would be coming from fresh off a temporary but likely permanent breakup. And as I had just told him a few nights before, I didn't want to keep burdening him.

It didn't take me long to get myself together, and Joss had agreed to meet for brunch at Bobby Sue's about an hour after I had sent my text.

When I went through the living room to get my keys, Creed was standing there with the suitcase he had rolled into town with, ready to pack. I might have guessed that a man who had been a nomad for years wouldn't settle down in Dove Creek for long.

"I'm not taking everything," he said. "Only what I need for now. I'll be back for the rest."

"I hope so. I truly hope so," I told him, trying not to get teary-eyed.

"For what it's worth, I have loved being with you. I never expected to find someone like you when I came back here. You're more than I deserve."

"It's worth a lot," I told him.

"I'll leave my key under the mat where it used to be."

And he would roll back out of town, leaving a gap in my life, a place I was supposed to hold open for him. If that was what was to be, I hoped he would find the answers he sought... soon.

I took three quick strides and wrapped my arms around his neck. "Take care of yourself. And come back to us."

He turned his face into my neck and inhaled long and deep. "Goodbye, Remi."

* * *

It was a cool, drizzly day outside the foggy windows of the diner. The gray damp was a perfect match for my mood.

"I'm so sorry to drag down what was meant to be a fun day," I told Jocelyn as I stirred cream and sugar into the heavy ceramic mug in front of me.

"Don't be silly. I'm flying high enough right now, literally nothing can drag me down. So I'm here to listen. And we'll go shopping and get some cute stuff and take your mind off things."

"I'm not so sure retail therapy works for me." I smiled a weak smile.

"How do you know if you've never tried?" she insisted. "You know, I thought Creed seemed a little off yesterday, but I wouldn't have expected *this*."

"Me, either. We've been a little out of sync ever since we saw Yescha and Michael, but I didn't imagine it would come to this. We had a good talk last night... I thought he was coming around."

The server placed two steaming plates in front of us, asked something I didn't register, and left us to it.

Joss lifted her knife and fork, but paused long enough to catch my attention. "You'll be okay, Remi. I know you will."

"I know I will, too. For now, I'll just mope around for a few days and get used to living alone again. It was only a few months, after all. I'm not even in love with him, not really. We aren't there yet."

"Oh?" she finished chewing a bite of fluffy pancake and washed it down with a sip of coffee. "I guess I thought that was one of those things you don't wait for. Either you are or you aren't."

"You sound like Gabriel," I told her.

"No one will ever stack up to Dominic unless you allow them the chance," she said, giving a direct look to my wedding ring. "I made a similar mistake, closing myself off for years, convinced that any other man I let get close would treat me like Jack did. And I was so wrong. When I finally took a chance, Dylan proved all of that completely wrong."

"So you're saying I should've given Creed more of a chance?"

"No, not exactly. If it isn't there, it isn't there. And he obviously has his own issues to go work out... Maybe after he works them out, it *will* be there. But my point is, you shouldn't discount the possibility that you'll find true love again."

I nibbled a piece of bacon and thought about what she was saying. Meg had told me something similar only a couple months before, after things had gone sideways with both Casey and Alex. I didn't think I was avoiding love, but I wondered if I was somehow sabotaging myself. Pursuing dead-end relationships out of a subconscious need to protect myself.

But until Valan was back in hell where he belonged, I would fear my love was a death sentence.

That wasn't a thought I wanted to continue to entertain, so I was shameless in changing the subject.

"So, have you and Dylan talked about wedding dates yet? Or is it too soon?"

Jocelyn's face brightened into a smile that rivaled the very sun. "We stayed up late last night talking about it. We're planning for the summer—probably early June before it gets too hot. But..."

She trailed off for a moment, the clouds rolling in across the radiant skies that had been her expression.

"But what?" I asked, concerned.

"My ex-husband's prison term is ending. He'll be out by Christmas."

"That's what Solomon came to tell you about the other night, isn't it? I'm so sorry. Are you afraid he'll try something?"

"Yes, Solomon came to tell me himself, since he was the one

who was instrumental in Jack going away in the first place. He said no threats were made or anything, but he wanted me to be prepared."

"I'd say these days you're pretty apt to plant him in the ground before he could even say boo."

"That's very true," Joss agreed, a certain edge to her tone. "And I have Dylan, who has been so good about all of it."

"You have all of us, too. Really. If he tries anything at all, we'll feed him to the hellhounds."

She grimaced, then her lips curled into a devious smile. "Honestly. Remind me not to cross you."

I grinned back. "You never could."

"I'm not afraid of him... not anymore. But I do worry about him trying to cause some kind of scene at the wedding."

I thought for a moment and came up with a simple solution. "There's a party barn out on the Blazing T Ranch. People use it for weddings all the time, and the property out there is gorgeous. You'd be out of the way where he would have to know about it to crash the party."

"That's perfect. We hadn't even talked about venues yet, but I'm sure Dylan would love it. I don't know why I didn't think of that."

"Sometimes when it's our own problem, we can't see the forest for the trees." I paused and finished the last of my coffee. "Now that we've talked over all our issues, are you ready to get going?"

"Yeah. It's high time I show you what retail therapy is all about."

Chapter 12

"If we stick with the same schedule, we'll kill ourselves," Casey said.

We were all sitting in the great room of Amasai headquarters, the updated first floor of the old farmhouse teeming with the stress of reconfiguring our rotation with Creed out of the picture.

"It doesn't change much," Gabriel argued. "Meredith already agreed to pair with Dylan, so if we switch to just having one person on backup each night instead of two, we should be fine."

Garret broke in: "And I can do double duty—act as backup some nights. Yescha gave me an ability, too, so I should use it. Stacey is getting the hang of the computer system and acting as dispatch, so she can be here to keep things organized like I do."

"I *hate* that idea," Aric said.

"I knew you would," Garret fired back, eyeing his twin with exasperation.

We weren't used to seeing the meeker of the two brothers stand up for himself, so instead of rushing to his defense, we let it play out.

"I can handle it. I've gone through the training just like everybody else here. Now that it's needed, I intend to put it to use."

Aric folded his arms across his chest. "Fine. But we're gonna talk about it more later."

"That's it, then," Hugo said. "We'll keep to the same rotation with Meredith taking Creed's place and pare down to only one on backup each night. Does anyone have any other objections?"

Words of assent went up all around—even from Casey and Aric—and the meeting adjourned. Hugo and Aric were out in the field that night along with Matt and Ty, Casey backing them up, so the rest of us lingered only long enough to ask after each other's plans. I didn't have any, for obvious reasons, and Gabe simply hadn't made any commitments. Jocelyn suggested that those of us who were free to go out for an impromptu celebration and (I suspected) to keep me out of the dumps.

"I can't tonight... I asked Viviana to stay with the kids only long enough to come for the meeting," Meredith told us.

I shrugged. "I'm in."

"Me, too," Gabe agreed.

"How about the Dirty Dozen?" Dylan asked.

"Maybe something more tame?" I asked. "I'm not in the mood for a dancefloor."

"Rack 'Em Jack's it is," Joss said.

As we crossed the wide front porch to hit the driveway, Gabriel asked me to ride with him.

"If you want to blow off some steam tonight, I don't blame you. But let me drive you."

He was right. A few shots of whiskey were likely to slide down and hit the spot, so I wouldn't need to drive. And I was more comfortable leaving my truck at HQ than in the bar parking lot overnight.

"Yeah, sure. Thank you."

"Don't mention it."

Settling into the passenger seat of the Chevelle at sundown felt like a night on watch, but I wasn't armed to the teeth. Granted, I was still packing heat and a couple of silver daggers under my jacket. Wearing layers was one definite advantage of the late season.

Jack's was fairly busy, but that was to be expected on a Friday night with no football game and after folks had been cooped up with their families for a couple of days. We were able to get a table in no time, though, and the bar was quick about getting us a pitcher of Shiner Bock and four frosty mugs.

"I'm just going to have the one, so I'll buy this round," Gabe said.

We set up at the pub table next to the pool table we had chosen, filling our mugs with ice cold amber. I scanned the crowd and recognized many of the faces from around town, but if any of them realized who we were, they said nothing.

"Who's gonna start?" I asked before I took a sip, then looked at my partner. "You and me?"

"Actually, there's something I wanna ask you, Rem," Dylan said.

Jocelyn slid off her chair and nodded Gabriel toward the racked balls. "We'll warm up the table, but you'll have to break."

She didn't pause to find out what it was my brother wanted to ask, so she must have either known or was in on the plan. There was no lingering curiosity before turning her attention to the game.

I swallowed another mouthful of Shiner and gave my attention to Dylan. "What is it you wanna ask?"

"Well… What would you think of us buying your house?" Before I could answer in the affirmative, he plowed on as though he had selling points ready in case I said no. "Now that Joss

109

and I are planning for the future, we're thinking long term and we've both saved for a good down payment. I know you don't want just anybody living in the house you shared with Dom, so I'm hoping if it's us, you won't mind."

He knew why I had hang-ups about putting the house on the open market—we had talked about them when I first offered it up to him to live in rent-free after he had moved back to Dove Creek. But to sell the home I had loved so much to him and Jocelyn was the perfect solution.

"Mind? Dyl, I'd be thrilled if the two of you wanted to make that house your first home. I'm happy to sell it to you."

He grinned ear to ear. "Awesome. We looked up the fair market value, and that's what we're prepared to pay. I know you, and I don't want you to make us some kind of stupid good deal just because I'm your brother."

"We'll talk more about that later," I laughed. "But if we call the bank on Monday, I'll bet we can close on the paperwork by Christmas."

Joss noticed our smiling faces and sidled up to Dylan, slipping an arm around him and giving him a peck on the cheek. "I told you she'd say yes."

"I was still nervous. Buying a house is a big deal."

Gabriel wrapped up his turn on the table and came to find out what was happening. "What did I miss?"

"We're going to be homeowners," Jocelyn told him with a smile.

"Something else to celebrate, then," Gabe said, raising his glass. "Congratulations."

"To Jocelyn and Dylan," I added, toasting them.

We all drank from our mugs, and while I had thought I'd need a few drinks to help drown my sorrows, I found that happy news and the good vibes around me lifted my mood far more. The truth was, I felt better than I should have. But I recalled looking at my wedding album the night before... While it was unfair to compare Creed to my late husband, I felt deep in my heart that something had been missing.

Gabriel interrupted my reverie when he set his glass on the table. "Not to rain on the parade, but I won," he grinned.

I looked over at the pool table. While Joss had come to talk to Dylan and me, he had disappeared every ball with a stripe on it into pockets.

I slid off the tall pub chair and snagged a cue from the rack on the wall. "Let's cut that winning streak to one, shall we?" I smiled back. "Your break."

My partner racked the balls and got ready to break, and I looked around at the crowd again. It was thinning out as the night wore on, but there were still plenty of folks milling about. I glanced toward the jukebox as an unlikely sight caught my eye... a head of dark, wavy hair and broad shoulders disappearing toward the door. It couldn't have been...

Gabe was lining up his shot when I made up my mind to investigate. "Hey, I'm just gonna run to the ladies' real quick," I lied. "Don't sneak any extra shots while I'm gone."

I made a break for it, sidestepping and 'excuse me'-ing my way through the throng. When I got to the main door, Creed was nowhere to be found. If he had been there at all.

Pushing through the entrance, I looked both ways on the sidewalk in front of the building. Nothing still. And he wasn't *that* fast.

I cursed under my breath, irritated with myself for jumping and running, when all I had seen was the back of some guy's head. Taking a moment to collect myself, I sucked in a few breaths of the chilly air but didn't get to do much collecting before I sensed someone too close to my personal space.

"Hey sweetheart, can you spare a smoke?"

I bristled at the use of the patronizing endearment, though my indignation gave way to high alert the moment I looked over my shoulder.

Vampire.

It was no secret what he was up to… Woman alone outside the pool hall, likely tipsy. Keep her alone, get her around to the back of the building. Bite.

Boy, was he in for a surprise.

He was too close—inside my defensible zone. To back him off, I played my part in the charade. I reached into my half-zipped jacket like I would if I were going in for a pack of cigarettes and retrieved the crucifix I wore. When I turned, I held it out and bought myself a few paces' worth of space.

When the vampire realized what he had gotten himself into, he bared his fangs and lunged forward. I reached behind me for my gun, but the bloodsucker was quick as a flash. He clocked me one in the jaw so hard it snapped my head around and I lost my footing. I stopped my face from its collision course with the concrete by landing on my hands and cushioning my descent.

My vision went blurry for a few seconds, but I held on to consciousness. Fighting my body's desire to stay down, I knew I was toast if I didn't find the strength to fight back. As far as my backup was concerned, I was in the restroom.

I swore to myself I'd never lie again, not even the little fibs like the one I had told Gabe.

Popping myself back onto my feet before the vamp could get in any ground and pound, I summoned the Holy Light. The practice I had done in the armory came back to me, and I created an orb of light almost as a reflex.

"No, not you..." the bloodsucker said.

He hadn't recognized me by looks, but he had obviously been warned about there being a light-wielder. Taking a step back, he shook his head.

I cast the light away from me, right at the heart of the vampire. The idea had been to stop him in his tracks, but he... disintegrated.

The front door to Jack's swung open from the inside at the same time the demon's host body imploded in a cloud of bright sparks and dark ash. I gasped as the crimson energy streaked away to Perdition, and Gabriel stopped short in surprise.

"I didn't mean for that to happen," I said. "I mean, I didn't expect it to... you know."

My partner looked in both directions from the door, then out across the parking lot, doing a visual check of our surroundings before turning his attention back to what I had done.

"Damn," he murmured, watching the ash settle. His gaze shifted to me, and curiosity was replaced by concern. "Are you okay?"

I put my hand to my jaw, pressing my fingertips gingerly where the vampire had hit me. The bone didn't seem to be broken, but I'd be left with some nasty bruising.

"Yeah, I think so."

My partner came closer, giving one more glance to the dusty leftovers of the demon before checking out my face.

"What were you doing out here?" he asked. "I thought you were in the ladies' room, otherwise I would've come sooner."

"I was on my way there when I thought I saw somebody I knew."

Not one hundred percent false, but he still eyed me with

113

skepticism.

"Do you want to call it a night? I can take you home, if you're ready."

"Yeah, let's get out of here. But I'd rather just go to HQ... I don't really want to be home alone right now."

"Of course, whatever you want. We should go tell Joss and Dylan."

We went back inside to the table and gave them a brief rehash of what had gone down outside. Dylan suggested making a sweep of the area to make sure there weren't any other bloodsuckers around.

"I'd be willing to bet he was a loner," I said. "He was trying to get some unsuspecting person alone, to feed."

"I'll text Hugo. Let them know you killed one here and ask them to keep an eye out in this area," Gabe said. "The four of us have been watching the crowd all night, so in here is all clear. Any others outside would have made themselves scarce after what Remi did to that one."

"I'm sorry to cut things short, when we were just getting started," I told Jocelyn and Dylan.

"Don't apologize," Joss said. "I'm already getting tired anyway, and you need to go get some ice on that."

With a confirmation from Hugo that he and Aric would check out the area around Rack 'Em Jack's for any more vamp activity, we left the bar. After I got into the passenger seat, I touched my jaw again and felt where it was already swelling.

"You should let Meredith look at that," Gabriel said.

"I will. But I'll just put an ice pack on it tonight and wait until morning to call her."

We pulled up at HQ, and Gabe walked me inside. Garret gave us a nod and went back to punching something into his keyboard, and Casey rose from the couch to greet us.

"Hey, I figured y'all were out for the night. What're you—? Oh. What the heck happened, Remi?" he asked, looking at my face. "Bar fight?" he asked with a wicked grin.

"That might've been better," I smiled. "I got decked by a vampire outside Jack's."

"Tell me you got him back."

"She fried him like an egg," Gabe said. "There was nothing left when I went to help."

"Damnnnn," Casey said, sounding impressed. "I didn't know you could do that."

"Neither did I."

Going to the kitchen to find one of the Blue Ice packs Gabriel had put back a few nights before, I found Stacey re-stocking the fridge with sodas.

"Hey, I usually do that when I'm on backup," I said. "It keeps me awake when I get bored."

"Same," she agreed. "Not that I'm not bored... Just needed to move around. I can't sit still for as long as Garret can, and being here helping him is the only way my mom will let me be involved."

"Not trying to undermine your mom, but aren't you old enough to decide for yourself?"

"Technically, yes, but seeing as I still live at home..."

I understood all too well the need to balance what you wanted with what was necessary.

"If it makes you feel any better, I'm pushing thirty and my mom still gives me hell about hunting. So yeah, it never ends."

We stood there smiling at our shared joke before Stacey realized I must've been in there for a reason.

"Oh, did you need something? Am I in your way?"

"No, I'm just getting an ice pack from the freezer."

Her eyes landed on my jaw, noticing it for the first time, and she sucked a breath between her teeth. "Yeah, that looks bad."

"I've had worse," I told her.

I found the ice pack I was looking for right in the front of the freezer since it hadn't had time to get buried again. Pressing it to the swollen lump on my jaw, I winced at the cold, but it was soothing once I got used to it.

"Let me grab you a couple ibuprofen while I'm over here," Stacey said. Since she had been going back and forth from the pantry to the fridge, she was right near where we stored the meds. "I was gonna go back in there and see if Garret needs anything."

I accepted the tablets she fished out for me and grabbed a bottle of water from the fridge. "Thanks. He was in there working on something when we came in."

We left the kitchen together and located all three men at Garret's desk, discussing the Crossroads, and went to join in.

"There are a few places that show up as hot spots when I overlay all activity—Creek Crossing, the county road in front of the Blazing T Ranch, and the east side of the lake. But really, we can't discount anywhere because look…" He switched the view of his heat map to where we could see every pinpoint instead of just the most heavy activity. There were blips covering the map of the area in and around Dove Creek like a bad case of chicken pox.

"So we're still shooting blind in the dark," Gabe said.

"I'm sorry this doesn't help more," Garret answered.

"No, don't be. We never would have known if you hadn't put together the data, and we can still try the places you mentioned."

"Is there a way to track the places where we're checking?" I asked. "You know, systematically eliminate them so that we're not duplicating efforts anywhere."

"That's a great idea," Garret said. "I can incorporate that capability in the mapping tool. I've taken this week to work out the bugs, so that won't take me long."

Casey gave him a firm pat on the shoulder. "That's awesome. This stuff is so far beyond me, it ain't even funny."

"Yeah, he's awesome. I'm good with this tech stuff and he blows me away," Stacey said.

Garret sat up a little straighter in his chair. "That's not true, but... I'm happy to help."

"Starting tomorrow night, we can pick our locations strategically, check them off the list when we're on our routes so we're not overworking ourselves," Gabe said. "Will you be ready by then?" he asked Garret.

"Definitely. I'll be ready by morning."

Our little gathering broke up as Stacey sat down next to Garret to help him, Casey went back to whatever he had been watching on TV, and Gabe and I went to the front door.

"You're sure you're okay?" he asked me.

"I'm sure... It was a very weird, very busy day, but I'm gonna be fine."

"And you'll go rest?"

"Headed up now, mommy dearest. You'd better go get some sleep, too. We're on tomorrow night."

"Yes ma'am, mission understood. Call me if you need me," he told me.

As I walked back through the sitting area, Casey caught my attention and asked if I wanted to join him.

"Nah, thanks though. I'm gonna go try to get some shuteye. But if anything goes sideways, come get me. I don't mind," I told him.

"Will do. Goodnight."

"'Night."

The upstairs of the farmhouse felt even emptier than I once thought it did without Creed in the room he had used, and even without Eden. We had filled the space for a while, and now it was back to just me occasionally using a room. But the feeling of being at ease still held me when I laid down in the twin bed in the corner. I was going to have to get used to being alone again, even if it did prove to be temporary, as Creed hoped. For the time being, though, I would seek out the comfort that the heart of the Amasai provided.

Chapter 13

The nights had grown shorter and colder. In the weeks since Creed left, I had gotten used to living in a quiet apartment again. There were times it was too quiet, but I had also begun to wonder if I wanted to hold open the space he had left in my life.

I hadn't heard a word from him. After that first night of imagining I had glimpsed him in Rack 'Em Jack's, there had been no sign of him. When I had tried to call his number a couple weeks before, it was no longer in service.

It left me to speculate what had happened to him. But I also thought maybe he had simply wanted to go back to his ways of traveling and never landing in one place for too long, and had tried to spare me from an ugly break-up. Whatever the reason for radio silence, I wasn't so sure we could just pick up where we left off if he did return.

There was enough to distract me in our search for the Crossroads and keeping the hellhounds at bay that I didn't ruminate on it too much. We had eliminated the busiest of the areas Garret had located on the map, and were going through all the other pinpoints a few at a time each night so we didn't overwork ourselves.

The longest night of the year came cold and clear, though in years past we hadn't known it to be a night of additional oddity or danger. Still, it was eerie to know that in the middle of it, we would be the farthest away from daylight we ever were.

Gabriel and I were on duty that night, along with Dylan and Meredith. Aric was in the armory with us, planning to fill more silver ammunition while he was on backup.

"Let me know if y'all need anything," he said, taking a swig of Dr. Pepper. "I'll be in here, passing the time."

"We will. Stay sharp," Gabriel told him.

The four of us went back to the house to review our maps against Garret's main Crossroads map. Chances were, we would have time to search some of the locations that hadn't been checked yet. He updated us with a few places where Solomon had open missing persons cases.

"Where's Stacey tonight?" I asked.

"She's out doing some Christmas shopping with her mom. They had some last-minute things they wanted to get. I told her I'm fine here since most of the work on the Crossroads map has been done."

I smiled. "I don't think it's the map that has her coming here every night."

Garret blushed and covered his embarrassment by going back to fiddling with something on the computer. "I'll let y'all know if I see anything strange tonight."

We filed out the front door just as the weak winter sun dipped below the horizon. It was so early that most folks were just getting off work. Since they likely had the same plan as Stacey and her mom—head to Westview for some Christmas shopping—we chose routes that would take us away from the flow of traffic in that direction. Gabriel and I went west toward Summer Valley, Meredith and Dylan sticking close to town.

There were plenty of people on the road at that time, so we had to keep to the speed limit to avoid annoying anyone. Even though we wouldn't see much that way, we could still watch for cars on the side of the road or any hellhounds that happened to cross our path again.

As the evening wore on, people were out less and less. It was only a few days until Christmas, so there were driveways full of cars where people were having parties or hosting their families for the holiday. Lights decorated most houses, and some went all out and did up their entire yards with the twinklers. In some ways, the festivities were good for us because all the extra light made for an easy scan of the landscape. And when people moved in groups instead of alone, it made them more difficult for the vampires to pick off without attracting unwanted attention.

We had made our loop and were making our way back toward Dove Creek when my phone rang.

"Hey, Garret. What's up?"

"Remi?" he said, his voice hushed and urgent. My heartbeat picked up before he spoke again. "Help... Get here quick."

There wasn't time for me to ask what the trouble was before he disengaged the call.

"Get back to HQ—fast," I told my partner.

Without questioning my request, he accelerated and picked up speed. Never was I so grateful he drove a muscle car.

"That was Garret, something's wrong. I'm gonna call Aric out in the armory," I said it even as I brought up his number to dial. "There must be a reason he called me and didn't use the comms."

Aric picked up on the first ring. "Remi, what's going on?"

"Get to the house now. Garret's in trouble."

"What? What do you mean?"

121

I could hear his breath pick up as he rushed out the door.

"I don't know, but I'm going to call Dylan and get him and Meredith there. They're closer than us."

"Understood. I'm hanging up now."

While I wasn't comfortable with Aric going in to a probable shitstorm alone, we couldn't leave Garret unprotected.

I relayed the same message to Dylan so that he and Meredith could get there even faster than us. They were going to send out the alert to bring in Hugo, Casey, and Jason and Ty. If there was something going down at headquarters, it was likely we would need all hands on deck.

The drive back felt like it took hours, even though it was only a few minutes. The Chevelle's engine screamed as Gabe pushed it as fast as he was comfortable going. And even moving at triple-digit speeds, we were the last to arrive.

Vehicles were parked haphazardly down the driveway in front of the old farmhouse, the urgency apparent the moment we got close: our headquarters was on fire.

That wasn't our only problem. Everyone who was already there was battling for their lives. Aric hadn't made it inside, which meant Garret was still in there.

Gabe had barely gotten the car into park before I leaped out of the passenger side. I drew an arrow and locked onto the vampire Meredith was fighting, and took the heart shot. Screw leaving them alive; we would deal with the repercussions of new hosts later.

I ran closer to the fray, taking myself into range of hitting them with the Holy Light. From behind me, gunshots rang out, and I glanced over my shoulder to see Gabriel had smoked a hellhound that was baring down on me. I felt him sticking close behind me, protecting my back so that I could let the light do what it did best.

Hitting the next bloodsucker I saw with a blast, he vaporized just like the one I had taken out at Jack's a few weeks before. I didn't stop to admire the show, instead finding another target. Aric was tangled with a female vampire who was dangerously close to getting her fangs into him, but her bloodlust proved to be my advantage. I cast an orb of Holy Light at her from behind, taking her out before she ever knew what hit her.

"Go!" I yelled at Aric. "Get Garret out of there!"

Hugo and Casey both looked toward the house, too, just then realizing the heightened urgency of the situation. I moved to eliminate their foes so they could help Aric, but couldn't get within range. Hugo lopped the head off the leech he was tangled with, so at least he was able to break free. He entered the farmhouse at a dead run, just behind Aric.

It was excruciating not to be able to get close enough to help, to have to watch from the sidelines as they ran headlong into danger.

My pain was only just beginning.

A familiar silhouette appeared against the backdrop of the flames. At first, I thought I was imagining him like I had at Jack's, but my eyes weren't deceiving me this time.

The bolt from a crossbow whistled by as my partner wounded a vampire on my flank.

"Rem, look alive! What's the matter?" he called.

I had tunnel vision as I zeroed in on Creed. Had he come to help us? How was that even possible?

But I watched him sneak around the corner of the farmhouse to the side, pointing back toward where we were all knee deep in the fray, giving orders to... a *hellhound*?

Without giving any more thought to the situation or contemplating the whys, I trusted what I was seeing. Sprinting through the brawl, I relied on my partner and my allies to cover me.

Halfway to him, Creed saw me coming. He turned tail and ran, gunning for the backyard between the house and the armory. I drew an arrow and aimed for the middle of his back.

"Stop or I'll shoot!" I yelled.

He stopped and raised his hands, then turned to face me. A smile slowly spread across his face.

"What in the hell do you think you're doing?" I demanded.

Chapter 14

"Don't you see? I've set you free," Creed said.

The smell of old wood and newer furniture burning filled my nose. Groans coming from the framing and metal roof nearly blocked out what he had said. Sparks rained down around us, threatening to catch us in the flames just like the old farmhouse. I barely tracked the raised voices carrying from around front.

The tip of my arrow didn't waiver from where it was trained on Creed's heart. It was a stand-off that took me back to a similar turn of events, when I had learned Creed wasn't who I thought he was and had been forced to shoot down his partner in the process.

And here we were again—another side of him showing itself. Another shocking revelation.

Fool me twice, shame on me.

I wished to God I had never found him and Eden in that house way back when.

"Free?" I questioned. My mouth felt dry, my tongue too thick and cottony. I swallowed hard. "I don't understand."

"This place." He waved a hand vaguely, as though the Amasai headquarters had meant little more to him than a nondescript shell of a building. And maybe it hadn't. "With it gone, you're free to choose where your loyalty lies."

"But I had chosen. I made that choice years ago. And again a few weeks ago."

"Things change. Surely you see that, now that we're together. You no longer have to fight for your dead husband because you can have me. I love you and I want us to be together, on our terms. We were meant to rule—not serve."

When those last words dropped between us like lead bricks, I knew.

Valan had gotten to Creed.

"No," I told him, fighting the quiver in my voice. "If you go down this path, you walk it alone."

Hurt showed itself in his dark eyes, momentarily blotting out the manic high he was riding. He shook his head, disbelief elbowing the fleeting pain of rejection aside like he couldn't grasp a reality in which I would respond with anything but devout appreciation for his acting as my liberator. I was supposed to be in awe of his attempt to break the Amasai from the inside out.

"Don't do this, Remi. Don't deny me."

The last time he had forced my hand, it had ended in a slap. This time, the consequences were so much more dire than an unwanted kiss.

Looking back, Creed had shown me exactly what he was capable of.

I answered him by lifting my chin and pulling my bowstring taut. "Give yourself up," I begged.

He reached for the gun in his holster.

"I don't want to shoot you!" I shouted.

Gabriel appeared at my right side, and Creed froze.

"She may not want to," he said, leveling his crossbow. "But I do."

My brother flanked me on the left. "What he said... only with an axe." He twirled both axes in his hands and set his stance.

If Creed so much as twitched a finger toward his weapon again, it wouldn't be up to me to spare him or not.

He glanced at the men on either side before zeroing in on me. "This isn't how I wanted this to go," he said, raising his hands in surrender.

I couldn't fathom it going any other way, except it not happening at all.

"That makes two of us," I said.

Gabe took a few steps toward him, I assumed to disarm him so we could turn him over to the police. He didn't make it that far, though, before the rushing wind gust sound came from behind.

Without a second thought, I dropped my bow and called up the Holy Light to a bright sphere in my left hand.

My partner recognized the disruption and stepped back even with me and Dylan, the level of his bow never wavering even as Valan materialized next to Creed. Dylan holstered one of his axes and brought up a palmful of Holy Fire.

Yescha had told me that any one of the three of us had the power to defeat Valan and here all of us were together. For the first time in all our encounters, I didn't fear the ancient vampire.

My newfound bravery wasn't put to the test, though, as he bared his fangs at us in a triumphant leer.

"Love what you've done with the place,"

He latched onto Creed and with that same wind-tunnel whoosh, they were gone.

I vanished the light within my grasp and retrieved my bow.

Without pausing to dwell on what had just happened, I took off for the front of the house.

"It's bad, Rem," Gabe said as he rushed to catch up to me.

"How bad?" I questioned, even as I ran.

"An ambulance is on the way. Hugo was hit when they were getting Garret out. Both of them are too much for Meredith."

Without asking more questions, I broke around to the front of the house. We were in the clear as far as our attackers went, but the consequences were just starting to show themselves. I snapped my bow into place on my back and slowed to a halt.

Garret was laid out in the grass, clear of the flames and debris, someone's jacket folded under his head as a makeshift pillow. He was unconscious, his skin red and angry in a few places, but the burns weren't extensive. Aric was next to him, sitting up but leaning heavily on his knees, his head down.

On the other side of Garret, Hugo lay prone and unconscious as well. Meredith was hovering over him, her face drawn and grim. She looked up when I approached.

"I got him breathing again. But the doctors will have to do the rest," she said, her eyes red.

I dropped to crouch next to her. "They will—he's going to be okay," I told her. "What happened?"

"He and Aric went in to get Garret out. It took a while, so Casey went in after them. They had almost made it when a rafter fell. If it weren't for Casey, both of them would be..." she trailed off when she couldn't say the word.

I glanced up to where Casey stood, his back turned to us. He had his face in his hands and his broad shoulders slumped. There was no heroic relief in his stance, only misery and defeat.

Reaching out, I took Meredith's hand in my own. There was nothing more I could say or do except stay to make sure they

128

made it into an ambulance without any further attacks. I took one of Hugo's hands, too, and said a silent prayer, begging for him to pull through.

I stood back up and heard sirens wailing in the distance, closing in by the second. There were a few dissonant notes, indicating a few different sources. The ambulances and firetrucks were all arriving together.

Dylan and Gabriel were both still standing guard, weapons in hand in case the vampires hit us while we were weakened. I went to Casey, putting a hand on his arm to get his attention.

"You okay, big guy?"

He dropped his hands from his face and nodded. "I'm fine." His voice was scratchy and quiet, but that was the only physical indicator of him being affected by the fire. "I tried to cover both of them, but I..."

"I know, Case. I know you did everything you could. Hugo and Garret are alive because of you."

He nodded, and I gave his arm a pat before returning to my brother and partner. A pair each of firetrucks and ambulances pulled into the driveway, parked in an organized formation, and moved in a coordinated effort to aid in our emergency. They had cut the sirens, but red and blue lights still flashed, casting odd shadows around the farmhouse. There was no hope for it to be saved—the firefighters' task would be to prevent the fire from spreading, not to save the old house.

"Creed can compromise the pawnshops. With Garret down and his computers here destroyed, I'll have to do a manual reset on-site."

Speaking those words was surreal. We had plans and safety nets in place for scenarios where a catastrophic event threatened our security, but I never expected to need to enact them.

"I'll go with you," Gabriel said. "It'll be dawn soon, but better to not take chances."

"Joss is at the downtown shop. I'll go to her," Dylan told us.

"Good," I agreed with him. "She knows how to do the reset. You go on ahead because it'll take you some time to get there."

"I'll call ahead and warn her," he said.

We exchanged a long look that didn't require either of us to say what we were thinking. It communicated all the *becarefuls* and *Iloveyous* needed.

Gabe and I waited to see Hugo and Garret off. Brooke, the paramedic who had picked up my dad and then patched a few of us up after the zombie attack, led the triage effort. She was checking out Garret and interjecting a few calming words to Aric here and there. Her partner was going over Hugo's injuries with Meredith, talking through it as he and another medic loaded him onto a gurney with careful, well-trained movements.

Casey made his way to where Gabe and I stood.

"I'll stay here and keep an eye on the place for a while," he told us.

Gabriel nodded. "Good idea. I'll text you the instructions for changing the passcode on the armory."

He seemed re-energized at the prospect of having something productive to do. And the firefighters would be at their task for some time yet, so he was doing us a favor.

"Let's get going," Gabe said. "I'll drive you."

I loaded up into his passenger seat and clicked my seatbelt into place. He pulled out and gave the emergency vehicles a wide berth as he took us down the driveway.

"Let's go to the shop here first. If anything's gonna happen, it'll be there. Creed won't attack us alone and there's not much night left."

My partner nodded and sped toward the heart of our little town. I picked up my phone and called the night shift manager at the Westview shop in the newer part of town and told him we had a security breech in our payment system. I knew it would be safer for him and any other employees to just not be there, so asked him to close down. Aric was scheduled to be there during the day, so we didn't have to worry about that. He wouldn't be working anywhere until Garret was out of the woods.

Gabriel swung into the Dove Creek shop as I was finishing the call. We both took a hard look around before getting out of the car, but the coast was clear. The same protective sigils and warding litanies that protected HQ protected the pawnshops, too, yet we had been compromised before by our living and breathing foes.

Worse than the brute forced of the Triple Six, though, Creed had a much more subtle way in. He had worked at all three of the shops and knew every security code and computer log-in we had.

The amount of damage he could do was unfathomable—he had already shown that.

We used the rear employee entrance and found Jackie in the office. She looked up from her work and flashed an automatic smile.

"Hey there, Remi." The smile faded when she took in our composed expressions. "Everything okay?"

"It will be," I assured her. "Listen, you're not in any danger, but our security system has been compromised. To be safe, I want you to go ahead and go home for the night. I'll let you know as soon as we're back in order."

"Does this have to do with the Amasai?" she asked.

Since we were forced out into the open, it was no use trying to hide it from her, but I wasn't sure how to answer.

"Yes," Gabe said honestly. "But like Remi said, you're not in any danger. We just need to do a few things to make sure it stays that way."

Jackie blew out a breath. "Okay, yeah... I get it. You two be safe. Let me know if there's anything I can do."

She got her purse from the desk drawer and hooked the strap over her shoulder. We followed her to the back door and waited until she was in her car. With a tentative wave, she pulled out of the parking lot and went on her way.

"What needs to be done?" Gabe asked when we returned to the office.

"Reset the alarm codes, computer log-ins, and out of an abundance of caution, the POS and payroll system log-ins. There's no way to know what all he might have tried to get into while he was working here. Speaking of... I have to terminate him as an employee." I allowed a harsh laugh at the last part.

I sat down in the desk chair and logged into the computer while Gabriel positioned himself in the doorway where he could see both into the main part of the shop and the rear entrance. He had been right to come; I could concentrate fully on what needed to be done instead of worrying about watching my six.

When Hugo had decided Jocelyn and I should be able to reset all of Dove Creek Pawn's security measures, we'd had Garret take us through the processes. I was able to work smoothly through it all—most of which was simply being able to follow the series of prompts. Others dragged on longer—two-step verifications that required texting a code and entering it.

I kept my head down and worked diligently, but had to move around and stretch my back after a while. I wasn't sure if it was the squeaky office chair or my spine cracking that caught Gabe's attention, but he turned when he heard me.

"You okay?"

"Yeah," I said. 'Okay' really wasn't the correct description for everything I was feeling, but my progress toward having the shop secure again was good, so that was what counted. "I'm almost done here."

I felt my partner looking at me, studying my profile.

"That's not what I meant," he said.

My fingers paused over the keyboard, and I turned my head to look at him.

"I can't talk about it now. Ask me again later."

He nodded. "Fair enough."

And he would. Once we had taken care of the shops and stopped by the hospital, I knew Gabe would bring up my wellbeing again. But for the time being, I needed to be last on the list of priorities.

"Is there anything else you should be concerned with? Would he have accessed employee records or stolen personal data?" he asked.

"I don't think so. He would've had to break into that on the job and we didn't get any alerts to that affect. Besides, it seems like he's more about just breaking apart the Amasai, not getting in to steal anyone's stuff."

"What makes you say that?"

"He told me he was destroying our HQ to make it so I'm free to choose. He's about the big gestures—burning our house down. That's why we have to protect the shops... We can't let him get inside, anywhere."

"And then there's your apartment... Where else does he know about?"

133

"Joss and Dylan's—what was my house," I said and thought back to anywhere else we had been that was even tangentially related to the Amasai. Remembering Thanksgiving, I blanched. "My mom and Hadden's house."

"It's okay," he reassured. "I'll call Dylan and warn them about going home. You call your mom and give her a heads up."

"None of us will be safe again until he's... out of the picture."

My partner read my misgivings, as clearly as if I had spelled them out in flashing neon.

"There may be a way to neutralize him without... you know." He paused and looked toward the front of the shop. "It's fully light out now. I feel sorry for him if he goes to your mom's alone, looking for trouble, but you should call her all the same. I'll go make some coffee and call Dylan."

As he disappeared into the break room, I palmed my cell phone and pulled up my mom's number. She answered after one ring and I started with the usual: "I'm okay, Dylan's okay," like all the other times I had called her early with a warning or bad news. I gave her the run-down about headquarters and Creed.

"One of these days, I hope to have you call me at dawn with some good news for a change," she told me, her tone dry as a bone.

"I hope for that, too," I agreed. "But for now, just promise you'll keep your eyes open."

"Always do, Remi-Jean."

The scent of fresh coffee alerted me to Gabriel's return to the office.

"I know. I've gotta get back to it, but I'll keep you posted. Love you, Mom."

"Love you, too."

I hung up the call and accepted the steaming mug Gabe offered. "Thank you."

"Any time. There was only the hazelnut creamer left in the fridge, not the French vanilla you like. Hope you don't mind."

"Not at all," I said before taking a careful sip.

"Is there anything I can help with besides keeping an eye out, or...?"

I shook my head. "Almost done here. Just need to reset the main password on the computer. Viviana will be the one taking care of Sofia and Daniel today with Hugo..." I trailed off, unable to speak the words.

"Rem?" Gabe prompted.

Shaking myself, I finished what I was saying. "Anyway, Vivi won't be in today, so we'll just stay closed since Sunday isn't a very busy day. I'll call Jackie and give her all the new codes for tonight."

He didn't call out my brief lapse in keeping to the task at hand. At least, not in so many words.

"We can stop by the hospital on the way to the other shop," he said.

"No, let's go straight to the shop. We won't do Hugo or Garret any good in the waiting room and I'll fail Hugo completely if I don't get everything secure."

"You haven't failed him at all."

His tone was too gentle. I expected someone to yell at me, like I was yelling at myself on the inside. *How could you have chosen such a man? Why didn't you listen to Yescha and Michael?* As it was, his gentleness and non-judgement brought tears to my eyes.

His hand landed on my shoulder, and I shook my head.

"Later. I'll break down later."

135

Chapter 15

The weak winter sunlight slanted across the parking lot, dappled by high clouds. I hadn't noticed how cold the night had gotten and the sun was no match for the chill in the whipping wind. Stuffing my hands into my pockets, I hunched my shoulders against it.

Our time inside had been long enough to allow Gabe's car to cool off, so it took a couple minutes for the heater to blow warm again. When it did, I stuck my hands in front of a vent.

"There are only a few days in the year when I'd really need it, but days like today make me want a parka for hunting," I said.

"True," Gabe agreed. "But I can't move as well in one."

Soon enough, the heated air blowing into the car's interior had me plenty warm. If it weren't for the continuing urge to batten down the hatches against another attack from Creed, the warmth and the white noise of tires on the highway might've lulled me to sleep. God knew I was tired enough.

When we neared the Westview city limits, I turned to Gabe. "Do you remember where the shop is in the newer part of town?"

By 'newer,' I meant the area of commerce and subdivisions that had been built out during the early 2000s. The heart of the city had shifted out of the old downtown, to the south and east, closer to Whitewing Lake. It bordered my mom's neighborhood, which had sparked the revival of the large and ornate foursquares.

In fact, it was the same freeway exit that led to my mom and Hadden's that Gabe took.

"Yeah, I haven't been inside in a while, but I pass by when I'm running errands."

From the exit, it took almost no time at all to reach the shopping center where the newest of the three shops in our chain was located. There were only a handful of traffic lights, and the only places that were busy at that time of the day were churches and donut shops.

Since nothing in the area opened until noon on Sunday, the pawnshop was already closed. It was the only location of the three not to maintain round-the-clock hours.

I scanned my key to get in the back door and disarmed the alarm system. This time around, we weren't as on edge since it was fully daylight and direct heat from Creed was unlikely. As we strode through the short hallway, Gabriel paused at the door to the employee break room.

"I'll do coffee duty again."

"Sounds great," I told him. "There's one of those single service brewers in there, so you won't have to make a full pot."

We went our separate ways—Gabe into the break room and me a few doors down to the office. I settled myself into the desk chair and logged into the computer. Since I had just gone through the rehearsed steps of the system resets, I started moving through them more quickly than back in Dove Creek. My only limitations were my typing speed and how fast the wi-fi moved.

I was grateful for the caffeine Gabe had been supplying; after sitting still for several minutes, staying alert was getting more and more difficult. My partner hadn't lit in one place since we had walked in, so I guessed he was fighting the fatigue, too. We still had a long day ahead of us.

"Dylan sent a text—he and Jocelyn finished downtown and are heading to the hospital," he said from the doorway.

"I won't be much longer here."

It took a little while, but by the time I finished, I was satisfied Creed would have to go through hoops if he wanted to ruin us financially. And by the time a hoop was breeched, we'd know.

The after-church crowd was filling the shopping center by the time we left, hustling from their cars into the chain restaurants that dotted the square. Clouds had gathered, blotting out what little sun there had been that morning, and the breeze blew chillier. I didn't blame people for huddling in their coats and jogging across the parking lot.

Putting my hand to my mouth, I covered a yawn as I settled back into the passenger seat and waited for the heater to warm back up. The trip to the hospital wasn't a long one—the sprawling Westview Memorial campus was on the edge of downtown, so it was only a matter of hitting the freeway and going down a few more exits.

I was glad we didn't have to go far, or else the throaty rumble of the Chevelle's engine would have lulled me to sleep. Despite the worry and unknowns, a pervasive exhaustion was elbowing its way in. If I didn't stay on the move, it would knock me down.

"How're you doing?" I asked my partner. "Sleep-wise, I mean."

One hand on the wheel, he glanced over. "I'm fine. For once, I got some extra sleep yesterday. You?"

"Tired, but I'll make it."

The hospital's main building loomed ahead, a visitor's parking lot sprawling before it. Gabriel pulled in and found an empty space not far from the front, so we wouldn't have to hotfoot it too far in the cold.

I thought of my last visit to the hospital when Casey had to spend a few days there. The very same elevator that had carried us up to the floor with the surgical unit took Gabe and me up again. The nagging feeling of dread was also the same—there was nothing I could do to change this outcome. Hugo's fate was in the hands of a capable surgeon... and God.

Meredith came over as soon as we got to the entrance to the waiting area, her face pale and eyes red. It was the first and only time I had seen a ripple in the surface of her serenity. I offered her a hug, and she held on for dear life.

"I'm so glad to see the two of you," she said.

"Is there anything we can do?" Gabe asked.

Meredith let go of me and wiped under her eyes. "Not really. He's still in surgery. They've updated me a few times to let me know he's doing fine, but... it's been hours. I can't imagine it's fine if..."

Her voice trailed off to a whisper and Gabe hugged her, murmuring something that must've been comforting because she gave him a wan smile and nodded as she let go. She dabbed the corners of her eyes with a tissue and visibly pulled herself back together.

"The kids are with Vivi?" I asked.

"Yes, they're at our house. What did you do about the shop?"

"Closed it for the day," I told her. "Even this close to Christmas, Sundays aren't very busy."

"Christmas... It looks like we'll be spending it here," Meredith said.

"Since it's only three days away, that seems likely," Gabriel agreed.

"Speaking of Hugo being here for several days… He told me a while back about the two of you taking over for him when the time came."

I opened my mouth to interrupt, to tell her now wasn't the time because he was going to recover. But she held up a hand and was resolute in what she had to say.

"For now, can you please keep us on the rails after last night's disaster?"

"You don't even have to ask," Gabe said.

"I have no idea what to do about our headquarters… How to fill the gaps in the rotation…"

"Let us worry about that. You focus on Hugo," I said.

She nodded and embraced us both again, wrapping her arms around Gabe and me at the same time. We gave her a squeeze in return and I found relief in being able to help, in being able to do something.

Joss and Dylan came over to us, cups of bitter hospital coffee in their hands.

"Want a cup, Mer?" Jocelyn asked her sister.

Meredith once again wiped under her eyes and smiled a thin smile. "No thanks. I've had enough."

"How is Garret?" I asked.

"He's up on the fifth floor. Aric and Stacey are with him," Dylan said. "They admitted him so they can monitor him for a day or two, but he's not in any danger."

"We'll go up and see them. Let us know if you hear anything about Hugo?" Gabe said.

We backtracked to the elevator to go up another floor and popped out into a similar corridor as on the fourth floor. Instead of a sign pointing one way for the waiting room, there was a sign with patient room numbers listed in blocs. We found the correct bloc for Garret's room and followed the arrow to the left.

Given that it was the holiday season, the hallways and nurses' stations were decorated with garlands, tinsel trees, and paper snowflakes—all manner of Christmas finery to cheer up the people staying there. There was also the occasional menorah or kinara outside a patient's door with LED candles to help them celebrate their traditions. There were more visitors coming and going than normal, but the noise level was low, as everyone remained respectful of those who were there to heal and rest.

Garret was laid up in a room on the corner, tucked away from the comings and goings. I knocked on the door softly, and Aric opened things up. Another round of hugs and *areyouokays* took place in the doorway before he told us Garret was sleeping.

Gabe and I went all the way into the room, closing the door behind us. In the chair next to the bed, Stacey slept, too, her hand in Garret's. They both looked so young—were so young—it made my heart ache. Their biggest problems should have been underage drinking and safe sex, but instead they were faced with the threat of death at every turn.

I rubbed the center of my chest and quietly cleared my throat. "How is he?"

"He'll be okay, in the end. Concussion, smoke inhalation, and second- and third-degree burns on his left side, thankfully only on fifteen percent of his body. They said they'll keep him here for a few days to observe his oxygen levels and make sure no infection sets in. He'll have a wound care nurse assigned to him when he comes home."

His voice was barely above a whisper, but the raspiness from having run into a burning building to help save his twin was obvious. So was his limp green mohawk and the brightness of the ink in his skin because he looked paler than usual.

"That's good news," I told him. "What about you?"

"I'm tight. They gave me oxygen and checked me out, then sent me on my way with some lozenges and a clean bill of health. I even got a nurse's phone number," he gave a little grin.

"Careful. Isn't that how Hugo and Meredith started out?" Gabe smiled.

Aric chuckled softly. "Didn't think of that. But since you mention them... Any updates on Hugo?"

"Not yet. He's still in surgery," I said. "Did you see what happened to him? Meredith said a rafter fell."

"He went in when I did to get Garret out. We got in and out pretty fast, but on our way out a huge beam fell and landed right on him. If it weren't for Casey, he would've... Well, I couldn't lift that beam, let's just leave it at that."

I pressed the backs of my knuckles to my lips, and Gabe gave my shoulder a light squeeze.

"Hey, it's okay," Aric said. "This is a great hospital, and—"

"It was Creed," I blurted.

"What do you mean?"

"He betrayed us," Gabe answered. "He set fire to headquarters and is in league with Valan and the others."

"Bastard," Aric spat.

He stomped across the small distance between us and gave me a fierce hug.

"This must be terrible for you."

I hugged him back, then waved off his sympathy. "Don't even think about that. It's Garret and Hugo who're paying the price of his betrayal."

Though I had been beating myself up from the moment I'd confronted Creed and was riddled with guilt, it was not the same as being laid up in a hospital bed.

I had clung to the hope that we would find our way back to how things had been between us in the beginning, once he found the answers he sought. Had longed for the certain, confident man who had attracted me.

And he had found his swagger again, alright. With Valan's influence.

Aric looked at his sleeping twin, then back to me. "You're right. There'll be no forgiveness this time."

"He made himself our enemy, so that's how we'll treat him. Period," I agreed, but said it with more conviction than I truly felt.

After the way Creed had held me at arm's length and then left, I wasn't heartbroken over him—I was plain pissed off. But what would happen if I had to face him in a fight? I wasn't sure I could do what needed to be done.

Gabriel looked at me in a way that told me he was probably wondering the same thing. His phone signaled a new text message, though, and he pulled it out to check it.

"It's Joss. Hugo is out of surgery. He pulled through and they're coming to speak with Meredith now."

"Keep me posted?" Aric requested.

"Of course," I told him. "Let us know if you need anything."

Gabe and I reversed course back through all the holiday cheer, to the elevator, and down to the surgical unit. Meredith was no longer in the waiting room, but Matt, Ty, and Casey had joined Joss and Dylan.

"The doctor is in there with Meredith," my brother said, pointing to the closed door of one of the counseling rooms just off the main area.

I told myself it could be good news. They came in and spoke

with the patient's contact person after every surgery, so the conversation happening behind that door wasn't necessarily bad.

We waiting for what felt like half a century but what was closer to half an hour. The surgeon's expression was inscrutable when she walked out, a mask of professionalism which left nothing to be gleaned, either good or ill.

Meredith's face was a different story. Her eyes and nose were red, her cheeks pale, and her visage tight, as though she were struggling to compose herself. She looked both grateful to have us there for support and like she wanted nothing more than to fade into her surroundings.

None of us spoke for a few moments, giving her space to share in her own time.

Joss went to her sister and they embraced. Soft words were spoken, mostly by Jocelyn, murmured phrases of comfort that seemed to help Meredith steel herself for what was to come. She stepped back and blotted her face with a tissue.

"Hugo is going to pull through," she said. The sigh of relief in our little group was audible. "He'll be... okay, except... He may never walk again."

There were soft gasps and whispered doubts such as "They can't know that for certain," and, "Surely not."

For my part, I was stricken silent. My feelings were a jumbled mess. Death, I had almost grown accustomed to. I knew how to deal with it. And a death of sorts had happened, but it was the end of an era rather than a life.

Hugo still had life, and in that, there was something to rejoice.

Meredith continued, "His spinal cord and vertebrae were severely damaged. They repaired everything as well as they could, but the injury is typical of those where ambulation is never fully restored."

"We're here," Dylan said. "Whatever you need, we're here."

"That goes for all of us," Matt added.

"He'll be in ICU for a while, so they're limiting his visitors, but I know he'll want to see you all once he's awake. I'm going in to see him now."

"Dylan and I will wait," Joss said. "That way you can go home for a little while and he won't be alone."

"Yes, please. I'll need to explain things to Sophie and Danny. And when he's allowed to have more visitors, I'll let everyone know."

We all agreed and left her with the promise that we'd be there in a heartbeat if there was anything we could do for her. The group of us were somber as we left. Casey, Matt, Ty, Gabe, and I rode the elevator down to the ground floor in near silence.

"What do we do now?" Casey asked as the doors opened and admitted us to the ground floor lobby.

"We take a few nights off to regroup," Gabriel said. "We're another person less in the field, and no Garret. No headquarters, though I have some ideas for that. Remi and I will monitor the scanners and call for help if we need it."

"Suppose they try to hit us hard, knowing we're having to recover?" Ty suggested.

"They're recovering, too," I told him. "Their chief concern now will be feeding and healing their host bodies or finding new hosts. But people move around in different ways during the holidays—it's harder to catch one alone, and that will be to our advantage."

Matt scrubbed a hand over his face. "I sure hope you're right. Let us know what we can do."

We disbursed into the evening, Matt and Ty together, Casey

in the direction of his Bronco, and Gabe and me back to his car. The wind had picked up even more, bitter as it whistled between the buildings. We all but ran in our separate ways.

"What did you have in mind for HQ?" I asked once we were inside Gabe's car, heater cranked as hot as it would go.

"It's a temporary solution, but I've noticed there's a warehouse over on the road that runs to Summer Valley with a 'for lease' sign on it. There are a few other places like that around, but it's the biggest and newest."

"That's a great idea. Let's go check it out as soon as they'll let us."

"It'll be dark soon. Where are you staying tonight?" Gabe asked.

I sat up straighter, the small amount of relaxation I had found in the heat and comfortable seat going out the window with another issue to solve. "With everything going on, I hadn't thought..."

"Come crash at my place."

"Are you sure? I don't want to impose."

My partner shot me a skeptical side-eye. "Nonsense. You're more than welcome. And I'll go with you first thing in the morning to get whatever you need. God forbid Creed were to ambush us tonight, we don't have much backup."

That was a very real possibility. Creed would know his chances of getting shot in the process of sneaking up on me were high, but would that be a deterrent? He had thrown that whole stop-at-nothing vibe back at headquarters, so I wondered if the promise of a bullet was enough.

On some level, I hoped he'd use the spare key and go clean out the rest of his things while I wasn't around. A confrontation could go nowhere good, but the question was, how bad would it get?

I was less concerned about myself than I was about anyone who might be with me—like Gabriel. Creed viewed the Amasai as a barrier to us being together, which left me with no doubt he was a threat to the others.

Chapter 16

"**R**em?"

I squeezed my eyes shut, rubbed them, then looked across at Gabe. "I'm sorry, what?"

"I was just saying, if you'd rather go somewhere else—"

"No, this is good. I was just thinking about... Well, it doesn't matter."

Gabe put on his turn signal as we approached the four-way intersection just before the town itself. Going right would've taken us to the swanky Iron Terrace subdivision and the left he took went toward the part of Whitewing Lake that narrowed and branched northwest from the main water.

Along that swatch of shoreline was another higher end neighborhood, but instead of sprawling houses, sleek condoes and townhomes looked out over the lake. The cluster of recent development was thoughtfully laid out. None of the steel, glass, and concrete interfered with the naturally beautiful views any more than it had to.

Dominic had been the architect that designed the modern homes, and it was somehow comforting to see a part of him live on in his work.

Gabriel's townhome was at the end of a row of the identical two-story dwellings. The garage door rolled up and away smoothly, allowing him to pull straight in. Neither of us opened our doors until it was back down, waiting until we were completely shielded from the elements to get out.

Everything about my partner's place was just how I remembered it: neat as a pin, spotless, swanky. I felt dirty by comparison just standing in the entryway.

As if he could sense my unease, Gabe offered up his shower.

"Do you want to go upstairs and get cleaned up? There's just the one full bathroom, so you can go first."

"You're not worried about me using up all the hot water? I might, given the state I'm in."

Dirt, smoke, and sore muscles all added up to a lengthy scrubbing session.

"Not at all," he said. "Instant water heater."

"Niiiice. I should've known," I smiled.

"When you go up, bathroom's on the right. The closet is connected and you can borrow some clean clothes if you want."

I glanced down at myself. "Thanks. I'll take you up on that."

While I had been there before, I had never been in the upper level. The master suite at the top of the stairs took up the entire second floor. The lights were on a motion detector and came on when I hit the top step. Gentle illumination came from recessed lights in the ceiling and was just bright enough to see, not blind. I glanced to the left and found a wall of glass. The pivoting doors in the center led to a balcony that ran the width of the room.

Walking over to take a better look, I decided the view alone would be worth the mortgage. Despite the cold, a breath of fresh air beckoned. I pushed the glass door open and stepped out onto the composite planks. My boots barely made a sound as I went across to the rail.

I watched dense clouds moving in across the lake, their low ceiling reflecting the lights from below as the sky darkened. The icy bite of the north wind stung my face and hands, but the discomfort hardly registered. An exhaustion so permeating it felt heavy and oppressive settled deep in my gut.

How could I have been so stupid?

Alone, in the quiet after the urgency of the day, I let my mind sink its teeth into what had happened. Flashes of our headquarters burning, the beautiful farmhouse going up in flames, Hugo's lifeless body, Garret barely breathing... All blurred my vision of the vast sky as though I were seeing it all over again.

Valan gloating about his victory, Creed standing alongside my mortal enemy, turning on us... on me.

Tears streaked down my face, going cold the instant they met the air. I brushed them away with a jerky movement as the door opened and shut behind me.

"You'll freeze out here." He draped a blanket around my shoulders and I curled myself into its warmth. "I didn't hear the shower come on, so I came to check on you."

"Looks like snow," I commented.

He glanced toward the low-hanging clouds and nodded. We so rarely saw snow where we lived, it would be something to be excited about under normal circumstances.

Nothing felt normal.

"You wanna talk about the weather," he said, sounding as exhausted as I felt.

"No, it's just..." I took a rattling breath. "I'm so sorry."

The tears came down again, uncontrollable. Gabriel opened his arms to me and I fell into them.

"God, Rem. What could you have to be sorry for?"

I sobbed into his shoulder, unable to form a coherent answer. Gabe stood there patiently, comforting, letting me cry and get it out.

"It's my fault," I sniffled. He shook his head and started to contradict me, but I continued before he could. "No, really. It was me who pushed Creed to figure out what he is. He didn't turn on us until after that."

Gabe handed me a handkerchief and pulled the blanket tighter around my shoulders. He cleared his throat like he was delaying what he had to say.

"I think we have to consider the possibility that he was never on our side in the first place. That he didn't defect to the demons, but was with them all along. You didn't push him to the other side. When Yescha told you what he is, he knew it was only a matter of time before you put it all together."

My stomach hit the floor. That possibility was so much worse. It meant I hadn't just been wrong—I had been played.

Burned. Like our headquarters.

"But I didn't put it all together, did I."

I turned away from Gabe and faced the lake. The frigid wind in my face was the only thing keeping me from hurling.

"I should have seen it coming. He was pulling away from me... Yescha and Michael even warned me off him, but I ignored them. I thought... Well, what difference does it make what I thought. I was wrong."

"We all were," Gabe said from behind me. "It was Hugo who invited Creed and Eden to join us, and I persuaded you to give Eden a chance. We both know how wrong I was there."

I turned my face to the side. "What are you saying?"

"That we all own this." He moved into my line of sight and met my eyes. "This is not on you. The blame is on Creed. He took advantage of our need and your kindness and trust."

"Oh, Gabe…" I wanted to tell him how grateful I was for him understanding, but words came up short.

He hugged me again and I held on tight. I was all cried out, but still so raw. There was nothing like the comfort of my best friend.

"Please don't blame yourself," he said against my hair. "We'll bounce back, like we always do. We'll make a new home for the Amasai. And you can stay here for as long as you need to."

We stood that way for a long time, me gathering my composure and Gabriel patiently allowing me the time to do so. His every breath was calm and even, the rhythm helping to steady me. The exhaustion I felt was beginning to ease, and the guilt that burdened me wasn't as cumbersome.

Still, I wasn't sure how to get over being the object of Creed's con job. Playing the fool left me feeling like an idiot.

"Hey, look."

I looked up at Gabe's quiet urging and followed his gaze to the sky beyond us.

Snow.

The tiny flurries sailed in on the breeze, harbingers of the fatter flakes to come. They were a beautiful sight against the dusky sky.

Even in the warm cocoon of the blanket and Gabriel's embrace, I shivered. It was then that I realized he was outside with nothing warmer on than his leather jacket.

I let go of him and took a step back. "We should go inside. I've kept you out here too long."

He shook his head. "It's fine. We can stay out here as long as you need to."

The pause lingered for a moment, as though there was

something else he wanted to say.

"Unless you're cold..."

"I am," I smiled.

"In that case," he said, turning to open the door, "after you."

I stepped back inside, back into the warmth of the upstairs bedroom. Closing the door behind us, Gabe shut out the cold.

"I'll go down and make us some hot cocoa so you can shower," he told me.

I had almost forgotten why I was up there in the first place, but there was blood on my jeans and my hair still reeked of smoke.

"Use anything you need. No rush," Gabe said before shutting the door.

The water didn't take long to heat up. By the time I piled my dirty clothes into a neat stack, steam billowed from behind the glass enclosure. I eased into the hot spray and my muscles relaxed.

It didn't surprise me to find high-end products on the tile shelf. The shampoo and conditioner were salon quality, and the body wash was from the nicest department store in Westview. Since Gabriel had such discerning taste, I came out smelling wonderfully clean rather than overtly masculine.

After toweling myself dry, I went into the closet to find something to put on. It was all dark wooden shelves and rods, sophisticated inset lighting, and organized to a tee. There were dress shirts arranged by color above slacks that coordinated, suits, silk ties, and expensive shoes down one side. Leather jackets, jeans, and heavy boots lined the other side. It was like two halves of the same man, visible in the contrast of his wardrobe.

There was a vertical line of drawers in the center of the side with the hunting attire, so I slid one open to peek inside.

Jackpot.

A neat row of t-shirts filled it, so I plucked a gray Aggies shirt from one end. It felt like a betrayal to my own alma mater, and the silly thought made me smile.

I found a cozy pair of plaid lounge pants in a bottom drawer and stepped into them. With the drawstring ties up, they fit nicely, if a little long.

Patting water droplets out of my hair, I went downstairs to find Gabe pouring hot chocolate into a pair of mugs. He looked up at me and smiled.

"Good timing."

I hung the towel around my shoulders and took the mug he offered me. The rich smell of chocolate and cream wafted up as I sniffed it. It wasn't the powdered instant stuff, that was for sure.

"Thank you," I said.

"I thought we could both use some rest tonight, then tomorrow we can go get whatever you need from your apartment."

"I can't sleep on your couch forever, you know," I took a sip of the cocoa. It was hot, just sweet enough, and tasted as decadent as it smelled. "Wow. This is perfect."

"Thanks," he told me. "And you won't be sleeping on my couch. You'll be sleeping in my bed. I'll sleep on the couch."

My eyes widened. I was already intruding on his hospitality enough, much less did I want to kick him out of his own bedroom.

"No, you can't do that. I won't let you do that on account of me being here," I insisted.

"I can and you will," he said, unyielding. His tone assumed that gentle firmness that meant his mind was made up. I could argue, but I wouldn't get anywhere. "It's not forever. Just until you find somewhere you like."

I blinked, afraid if I thought too hard about the kind gesture, the tears would start up again.

"I don't know how to thank you."

"You don't have to. That's what friends are for. You've had a tough few months, so if there's anything I can do to make things easier for you, I'm happy to do it."

I set my mug on the granite counter and hugged him tight enough I was surprised bones didn't crack.

"Thank you," I murmured.

He was right—the last months had taken their toll. The heaviness and overwhelming feeling of exhaustion were the products of setback after setback. Failure after failure.

But no matter how many times I got knocked into the dirt, I had to get back up. Knowing I had friends who would be there with a hand to pull me back onto my feet would always keep me trying.

"You okay?" Gabe asked.

I realized I was still clinging to him, so let go and took a step back. "Yeah... sorry."

"Nothing to be sorry for."

His expression of concern was replaced with a smile when he picked up my mug and handed it back to me.

"Come here. I want you to see this."

I followed him out of the kitchen and across to the living room. The entire wall that faced the lake was nothing but windows. He touched a button on a remote control and it killed the lights.

Without the light from within, we could see out into the darkness. The faint glow of exterior lights from all the houses around Whitewing Lake illuminated the swirling snowflakes.

It was magical.

"Beautiful," I whispered.

"It really is, isn't it," Gabriel agreed.

We stood in silence for several minutes, just watching the winter storm. It was utterly peaceful, finishing our hot chocolate in the quiet and warmth. I was never more grateful that Gabe isn't one to fill silence for no reason. The calm gave me a few moments to re-center my thoughts.

My partner was right: Creed was the one to blame for his part in our troubles, not me.

I made up my mind not to wallow in misery. Tonight, I would rest. Tomorrow, it would be time to plan.

Chapter 17

"I know what we can do!" I shouted as I bolted down the stairs.

Pale gray light through the front windows lit the lower level of the townhouse, so my rush to find Gabriel wasn't hampered by trying to figure out how to get the lights on. The couch was empty when I reached the living room and I spared only a brief glance for the view beyond, gorgeous though it was.

"Gabe?" I called.

He appeared at the mouth of the kitchen, cup towel hanging over one shoulder and a spatula in his hand. I would've found him quicker if I had followed my nose rather than relying on my eyes.

"In here," he said. "Everything okay?"

I hurried over, skidding to a halt on socked feet. "More than okay. I have an idea."

He motioned toward a place at the bar. "Sit. Tell me."

I perched in one of the tall chairs at the raised granite bar top. It faced the range, so Gabe was able to give me his attention while he flipped pancakes. Which, by the way, smelled like heaven.

"I want to give my land to the Amasai. There are nearly fifty acres and it's covered in trees. The best part is, Creed doesn't know about it, so it'd be a secret. We could build our new headquarters there. Well, *I* wouldn't be part of building it, but you know what I mean by we…" I trailed off when I realized I was babbling.

Pancakes plopped onto a platter as Gabe took them off the griddle. His expression was one of genuine consideration.

"It's a great idea," he told me.

Turning to the coffeepot, he filled two mugs and fixed mine how I like it.

"Are you sure that's what you want to do with it? You've been saving that land for a while," he said as he slid one of the cups of coffee toward me.

"Exactly. And it's just sitting there, waiting to be used." I paused and took a sip. "You always get it right," I said of the cream and sugar.

He set the platter of steamy pancakes in front of me, then took another large plate out of the warmer piled high with bacon and eggs. My nose reminded my stomach just how hungry it was, causing it to unleash a ferocious growl.

"You didn't do all this for me, did you?" I asked.

A plate, utensils, and a napkin appeared in front of me, then Gabriel set his own place.

"It was partially selfish," he smiled and walked around to the sitting side of the bar top. "I woke up starving since we never stopped to eat yesterday, but I don't cook like this just for myself and I enjoy it."

"It's no fun cooking for one," I agreed. "But this is enough for an army."

Gabe laughed. "I forgot how far pancake batter will go. Back when I learned to cook, it was for the whole family." He grew more serious. "You know how it was with my dad after my mom died... So there was a lot of trial and error but I learned."

I thanked my lucky stars I had a strong momma who hadn't collapsed when my dad left. Things hadn't been easy, but we were always taken care of. I couldn't imagine losing what amounted to both parents in one blow.

"I guess we've both done what we had to when the rug was pulled out from under us. I'm sorry I brought it up..."

"You didn't—there's nothing to apologize for. I was old enough and had resources, so I have nothing to complain about," he said.

I would've argued that resources in the form of a great house and more than enough money were no substitutions for parents, but I sensed I'd only be beating a dead horse. It was also my own way not to wallow in the past, so I respected his boundaries.

Gabe motioned for me to dig in, so I filled my plate with a little of everything. Since I didn't want to pester him any more about why there were approximately twenty pounds of pancakes for just the two of us, I went back to our needed conversation about a new Amasai HQ.

"So is it possible," I asked, slathering butter onto a short stack of pancakes, "to build a new headquarters?"

"More than possible. There's only one issue I see."

"Money."

"Yes. We have some, but not enough."

"Maybe if we sell the land HQ is—was—on. It's a strong market," I said between bites. "How *do* you get eggs to melt in your mouth like this?"

"Butter. Lots of butter," he smiled. "I think you're on the right track with the land sale."

I hoped I was. Incidentally, I had just come into a sizeable amount of capital with Dylan and Jocelyn buying my paid-off house, which meant between that and what my dad had left me, I was building quite a nice little nest egg. Putting a portion of that toward helping with a new home base for us wasn't out of the question, but I hadn't yet decided how much was prudent and didn't want to be irresponsible.

No matter what, it would be a team effort. We all had something to put toward rebuilding, and Gabriel's contribution was obvious.

"You'll design it, right?" I asked him.

He tapped his temple. "I already have a few ideas. In here and on paper."

"Of course you do," I smiled. "Now, we just have to secure a place in the meantime."

"Let's finish breakfast, then we'll drive out to that warehouse and get the phone number that's listed on the sign, if the roads aren't too bad. We can stop by your apartment, too, and get anything you need."

I nodded and finished chewing a piece of bacon. "But what time is it?" I asked. "Don't you have to go to work?"

"Already had the day off," he said. "I usually shut the office down and give everybody the week of Christmas off."

"That's really nice of you," I said, dabbing my lips with a napkin.

Gabe gave a little shrug. "It's what's right. Barring any urgent requests, we don't have much going on. Might as well let everyone spend time with their families."

I drained the last of my coffee and thought about how little we all did life together. We were a tight-knit group and knew a lot about each other, but that was mostly from hanging around headquarters together and the occasional night out. Then again, there wasn't much 'life' to do outside of that.

"Do you want more coffee?" Gabe asked, interrupting my musing.

"Yes, but I'll get it," I said, hopping down off the bar chair. I didn't expect him to wait on me hand and foot just because I was a guest in his house. "Do you want more while I'm up?"

"Please."

I went around to the maker and poured us both a fresh cup, leaving his black like he liked it. I set it back down in front of him before going back to the fridge for the creamer.

"Thanks," he told me. "When we're finished here, your clothes from yesterday are hanging up in the laundry room. Not that we're in a rush or anything, but I thought you might wonder."

I sat back down next to him and shook my head. "I don't want to wait around while there's stuff that needs doing, you're right. And thank you—I didn't even notice they were gone."

"I snagged them when I went up to get a shower before you went to bed and washed them with mine. I mean, you can't just wear my pajama pants around in public," he grinned.

"Who says?" I scoffed. "Isn't pajamas-as-clothes a trend these days?"

We shared a much-needed laugh, finished our breakfast, and got dressed. No pajama pants.

The coat closet downstairs was rigged out to store firearms and other weapons, and I had stowed all of mine in there alongside Gabe's the night before. I retrieved only the forty-five I carried on the regular—silver broadheads and wooden stakes were superfluous in the light of day.

As Gabriel backed his car out of the garage, we were plunged into a world of frosty white. The roofs, trees, and ground were blanketed in snow right up to the water's edge. The sky was still a pale gray, the milky smooth winter clouds blocking out the sun. There were darker clouds on the horizon, threatening more of the white stuff.

"I don't remember the last time we had a white Christmas," Gabe commented.

It was a rare thing to behold. Even more rare to have snow stick around for more than a day. The sub-freezing cold seemed to promise we were in for it this year.

"Let's go get my truck. I have a feeling we'll need the four-wheel drive on the back roads," I said.

"I think you're right."

He steered us toward the heart of Dove Creek and it took a little longer than usual to get around. Even so, we were pulling up at my apartment building within five minutes.

I went to dash to my truck to start it and let it start warming up, then paused.

"I'll just run inside for a minute and get a warmer jacket," I said.

Gabe undid his seatbelt. "I'll go with you."

Confused for a moment, I started to ask why but answered my own question before it hit the air. Right. Creed knew where I hid my spare key.

I got out and hurried to the truck, got in, and fired it up. We wouldn't be gone long, so I left it running and went with my partner up the stairs to my door. My cold fingers fumbled with the key for a few seconds before sliding it home and clicking the bolt free.

Gabe stopped me with a hand on my shoulder. "Let me go first."

The protest that was ready on my lips died as soon as I thought about it. He was far more likely to pull the trigger if it came to that. I let go of the knob and backed up enough to let him in front of me.

Handgun drawn, he eased the door open and kept a wary eye. I put my hand on the grip of my weapon, but didn't pull it. Staying close to Gabe, I looked around and found nothing wrong.

Glancing through the living room, I noticed an empty spot on the bookshelf where Creed had kept his books. The blanket he liked for watching movies was missing from the basket. Things he had left behind with the intent of returning for them.

"He's long gone," I said.

Gabe looked at me sidelong without lowering his gun. "How do you know?"

"I just do. But we'll do this your way, to be safe."

I followed my partner as he cleared each room, watching his back. Even with my reasonable certainty of Creed's absence, dropping our guard was a bad idea.

Our course finished in my bedroom, which was just as well, since my heavier coat was in the back of the closet.

Gabe slid his Sig back into the shoulder holster and pronounced us to be in the clear before turning to me. "How did you know he was gone?"

I beckoned for him to follow me as I went to the closet door. Pulling it open, I found what I had expected: An empty space on the rack where Creed's clothes had hung. It made my point for me, so I simply showed Gabe.

"That's how. His things were gone from the living room, and dollars to donuts there's an empty drawer in the bathroom. He hadn't taken everything with him when he left—just enough to travel light."

In a way, it creeped me out that he had been in my space alone now that were were on opposite sides. But if I were being honest, it made my skin crawl to have been with and so intimately connected my life with someone who would act as Creed had.

"Everything alright?" Gabe asked. "You look a little disturbed."

"You're right about me moving out of here. Even if it weren't for safety's sake, I just don't want to be in this place anymore."

In danger of tearing up again if he kept looking at me with earnest concern, I disappeared into the back of the walk-in closet to switch out my leather jacket for a parka. It was a big-fluffy goose down affair with a faux fur-trimmed hood, the kind of coat that was a once-a-season type thing in Texas. I found matching black gloves in the pocket, but waited to put them on since I still had to deal with locking up.

I draped the leather jacket over my arm, just in case we ended up seeing action since I couldn't move like normal dressed like a toasted marshmallow. Gabriel came with me out of my bedroom and to the front door.

"I won't need much—just a few clothes to get me by. It won't take me long to pack later," I told him.

"Don't worry about it. We have all the time you need."

I nodded and opened the door to walk outside. After locking things up, I pulled on the hood and gloves and felt much less like scurrying to my truck now that I was properly outfitted for the cold.

The old diesel was nice and toasty when we climbed inside. I put it in reverse and told Gabe my plans.

"I think once we get past Christmas I'll sell all the big things in my apartment to make it easier. I'll call the landlord, too, and break the lease. He shouldn't give me too much hassle since he'll have somebody on a wait list for sure."

"That seems a little drastic, selling your stuff," he said.

I smiled a little. "Nah, I'm not particularly attached to any of it. I bought all the furniture when I moved in just because it looked good and fit the space. I'd like to do the same when I find somewhere new."

"In that case... I was thinking you might've been going scorched earth. Anything Creed touched was out."

I laughed as I turned off the main highway onto one of the two-lane county roads that ran out to the even smaller community of Summer Valley. The busier, bigger thoroughfares had already been plowed and cleared, but the side roads were still covered in snow, as suspected. I downshifted and took it slow, but the truck handled it well since there was no ice on the surface below.

The building in question came into view, its roof covered in white but the sides were visible and a sensible khaki color. It was relatively new and had housed only one business that I knew of and all the signage was still there: Sumner Pipeline Co.

I wondered what had happened to them as I pulled in the drive and stopped at a locked gate. But just as Gabe had said, there was a 'For Lease' sign hung on the chain link and a phone number was listed right below the bold lettering.

Gabriel was already typing the number into his phone when I put the truck in park.

"It's mid-morning," he said, putting it on speaker. "I'll try calling now and see if I get anyone."

I nodded and waited while the other line rang once, twice...

"Hello?"

"Good morning. I'm calling in regards to your building that's for lease," Gabe said, sounding so polite and professional I doubted he could be denied anything he asked.

"Why, yes," the man on the other end of the line perked up considerably. "It's still available, Mister—?"

"Wyatt," Gabe supplied. "When would be a convenient time to have a look inside?"

The older man chortled. "You one of George Wyatt's boys?"

"Yes sir, I am."

"Well I'llbedamned. I used to work for George before I started my own business. Name's Russell Sumner. Tell ya what—I've got some time now if you wanna meet there."

My partner and I shared an optimistic glance.

"We're here since we stopped by to get your number on the sign, but don't feel obligated to get out in the bad weather, Mr. Sumner."

"Naw, it's no biggie. I live one driveway down. And it'll give me an excuse to get out of more baking," he added in an undertone. "Gimme five minutes and I'll be right there."

The call ended and I was astonished by our good luck.

"Glad you tried," I said. "Him knowing your dad seems to have helped."

"Give him thirty seconds after he meets you, and I'll bet he figures out he knew your dad, too."

"That wouldn't be a big surprise," I smiled.

We chatted for a few minutes about how big we thought the floor plan might be, based on the outside. Decided on an upper threshold for what we could afford in the Amasai budget for a monthly payment. And by the time we had landed on the yay or nay zone, Russell Sumner was pulling into the driveway next to us.

He wasn't in a shiny new truck how most oil business owners were; his was a Ford very similar to what I drove and not far off on the year model. It was even the dull, rusty-hued red that seemed part and parcel for that aged truck, not a glossy fresh coat of paint like Dom had done when he bought his.

We both left our trucks running when we got out, and Gabriel crossed in front of mine to meet our potential landlord with a handshake.

"This is my partner, Remi Hart."

As the older man offered me his hand, bushy eyebrows lowered. "That wouldn't be short for Remington, would it? As in McCoy?"

Gabe flashed a grin and whispered, "Make that ten seconds."

"Yes, sir," I said, stifling a giggle. "That's right."

He clapped his hands together. "Well, I'll be. I remember going into John's shop not long after you were born and having a good wonder about naming a baby girl after a gun, but he was so proud of you. I'm real sorry he passed."

The fond memory he shared brought a smile to my face—not tears to my eyes, for once.

"Thank you, Mr. Sumner."

"Y'all can call me Rusty. Now, let's get this gate unlocked so we can get out of this cold and take a look around."

Once he got things opened up, Gabe and I followed him up the rest of the driveway to a wide overhead door with a smaller metal door inset next to it. After another quick unlock, we went in through the smaller door.

The space inside was massive and completely clean. Off to the left, there was a wall that divided the building at about the two-thirds point, with a hallway in the middle of it.

"This was the warehouse area," Rusty indicated the expanse of open floor plan. "I didn't have it climate-controlled, but that wouldn't be hard to do since it's well-insulated."

I pictured the contents of our armory relocated to that very area and nodded.

"Now back here are a couple offices, bathroom, facilities, and a break room," he pointed down the hallway and waved us to follow. "All this is under heat and A/C, so it stays comfortable year-round. And the kitchen's not quite a full kitchen, but it's nice."

It was nice. All of it had a feeling of being fairly new, and while it wasn't homey like the farmhouse, we could still be comfortable there.

Gabe asked the pertinent question about how much the monthly rent would be, and Rusty came back with a number that was lower than expected.

"Since I sold up to that big outfit based in Houston, this place has been empty and I don't want it to fall into ruin. I keep up with the maintenance, but there's nothing quite like having folks in and out regularly. And there's not many other businesses in and around Dove Creek that need or can afford to be in here."

"I'd be remiss in not telling you we're not here in a business capacity," Gabriel said.

"Oh? Well, even if you intend this place for personal use, all that's important to me is that it's cared for and the rent's paid," Rusty chuckled.

Gabe hesitated and glanced at me as though he were unsure of divulging our true need for the building.

I spoke up, "It won't be for personal use in the way you're thinking. You know how Dove Creek was overrun by zombies a few months ago." It wasn't a question, and I didn't wait for confirmation because there was no chance he had forgotten. "We're part of the group that fended off the attack. Our headquarters burned night before last and we're looking for a new home."

With all the cards laid on the table, Rusty stuffed his hands into the pockets of his Carhartt jacket and examined his boots.

"I've heard talk that there's been an organization of regular folks protecting the town for a while now. Never knew any names. I remember back forty years ago when we all thought this'd become a ghost town. Always knew there was somethin' not quite right, but it's been better for a long time. I reckon we owe that to you and we owe you a debt of gratitude for what you did a few months ago…"

I could sense the 'but' coming before it surfaced.

"But I can't risk having your operation not four hundred yards from my home," he hooked his thumb in the direction of his house. "I'm sorry, I can't help you."

At a different time, I would've argued, but since we had just been burned out of our original place, I knew we couldn't guarantee a similar situation wouldn't spill over to his home.

Gabriel tried with the logic I couldn't summon: "We take precautions—make sure we're never followed, put up protections, keep a low profile. We aren't amateurs that'll get you killed."

Both our phones went off with a text at the same time. I glanced at it to see it was a message from Meredith—Hugo was awake.

I didn't have to tell Gabe to cut it short; he smoothly wrapped up our talk with Rusty Sumner.

"We have something urgent to attend to. No hard feelings—we understand your concerns," he said, offering his hand.

The older man accepted it with a firm handshake. "Y'all take care of yourselves."

The sting of disappointment was easy to ignore in the face of the small victory of Hugo regaining consciousness. It was, after all, the first place we inquired about.

I all but jogged to my truck, and Gabriel was right there with me. We jumped into the toasty warm cab and I threw it into gear as soon as our seatbelts were in place. As much as I wanted to hurry, though, the snow made a mad dash to Westview impossible. I settled for slow and steady—sliding off the road wouldn't get us there any quicker, and even the big diesel I drove wasn't infallible.

There wasn't much of anything we could do, but I could sense Gabe's need to be there for Hugo as keenly as my own. He would have a long row to hoe, whether or not what the doctor said proved to be true.

On two feet or in a wheelchair, he was still our leader.

Chapter 18

"I'm so sorry," I croaked through a constricted throat.

Hugo was still in ICU, his number of visitors limited, so it was just the two of us. They had taken out the breathing tube and promised a regular recovery room the next morning if his vitals remained stable.

"There's nothing for you to be sorry for, *mija*. Creed had us all fooled."

His voice was hoarse, too, but from a tube having been rubbing up against his throat, not tears that threatened to fall.

I knew he couldn't talk much, and I didn't want to take up a lot of time since there were others waiting to see him. So, I didn't argue the finer points in the who-was-to-blame debate.

"We're holding onto hope... that you'll be back," I told him.

"If I am, by some miracle, it will be a very long time."

One big, fat tear escaped and rolled down my cheek.

"I've made peace with it. And I have you and Gabriel to rely on," Hugo said.

"We won't let you down," I promised.

"There's something I want to give you," he said and tilted his head in a tiny movement toward the table next to the hospital bed. I followed his eyes to where he looked. "That rosary. Take it."

"The one you always carry in the field?"

"It has warded off many vampires and exorcised a few demons—you'll need it now more than I will."

As he spoke, I picked it up and felt the smooth beads pass through my fingers. It was pure silver and weighty, as if showing its own significance through shear gravity. I had never held one before and was struck by the solemnity of thousands of prayers and recitations because surely that was how many had been said over it.

"Am I even allowed to have one of these? I grew up Methodist, you know."

Hugo made a sound that would have been a chuckle were he healthy. "For what you'll be using it to do, yes."

I squeezed the crucifix piece in my palm. "I'll take good care of it."

"I know, *mija*."

When I quietly shut the door behind me, only Meredith and Gabriel were left in the small waiting area. I tucked the rosary into the inner pocket of my jacket and joined them.

"He seems to be in good spirits, all things considered," I said.

Meredith nodded. "He truly believes there's a plan for us all, so he takes comfort in that."

"But you're worried about him."

"Yes, but…" She paused and blinked hard a few times. "As long as he's alive, we can get through anything."

She stopped abruptly, as though realizing she might cause me pain with her honest relief. If she was going to say anything about it, she was interrupted by Gabe and I both hugging her. There had been a few agonizing hours the day before when it wasn't clear Hugo would hang on to life, so I wasn't upset by it. I was glad for her not to know what it felt like to lose the one you loved above all others.

Stacey came around the corner and hesitated, worried she was intruding on us. I let go of Meredith and waved her over.

"Hey Stace."

"Hey. Aric said Hugo's awake."

"He is," Meredith said with a small smile. "How's Garret?"

"Ready to break out. Just waiting on the discharge order to be signed off on."

Meredith got to her feet and patted Stacey's arm. "I'm so glad and I'll tell Hugo the good news." She went to the door and paused before pushing it open. "If there's anything you need me for…"

"Don't worry about us. Focus on your family," I said.

She gave a nod before disappearing into Hugo's room. There was so much right in front of them to deal with, the last thing she needed to be doing was mixing it up in the field or being called upon to heal injuries. For a while at least, we would have to go back to recovering the old-fashioned way.

"I came down to find you and offer to help," Stacey said. "I know how to do what Garret does and even though he's going home, he needs rest for a few days."

"That would be helpful," Gabe told her. "What kind of equipment do you need?"

"Nothing. He has a full set-up at their house. You know Garret—he has a backup for everything."

"Never have I been more glad about that," I said. "We aren't doing any official rounds until after Christmas, but Gabe and I will be available if you catch anything that needs our attention."

"Dad and Ty would be glad to back you up if you need it," she offered.

Gabe nodded. "I'll text them later."

"I better get back up there. Don't want to keep them waiting in case the orders came through."

"We'll stay out of the way so we don't hold y'all up, but give Garret our best. Let us know if you need anything, even if it's not Amasai related," I told her.

"I will."

She turned to go back the way she'd come, then smiled and waved over her shoulder.

"It's nice to have young talent in the group," I said.

"It is," Gabe agreed. "It's what will keep us going in the long run."

* * *

The day was darkening early yet again as the clouds had clung to the sky without a single glimpse of the blue beyond. Flurries had fluttered about on and off, but it was snowing again with renewed strength as we pulled up the driveway to Gabe's townhome.

I had packed one big suitcase with as many things as I thought I'd need, including something nicer than hunting clothes for Christmas. While we were at my apartment, I had also snapped a few photos of the bigger pieces of furniture to list for sale online. There weren't any apartments or houses immediately available—no surprise given the time of year, so the less I had to move and store, the better.

We were having even less luck finding a new place for the Amasai. Like me, our team was also uprooted. Gabe and I had decided we could meet in the armory as needed, but only temporarily. We were vulnerable there.

Gabriel hauled my suitcase out of the bed of the truck and

to the door for me. He punched in the code on the keypad and opened the wide front door.

"Feels weird coming in this way," he commented. "I always go through the garage."

I hesitated at the threshold. "I know I've already asked a thousand times, but you're sure I'm not in your way? Don't you have plans for Christmas?"

He set the suitcase on the polished hardwood and turned to look at me. "Are you trying to heat the neighborhood?"

Rolling my eyes at him, I shut the door with a click. "I thought you had to be a dad to say stuff like that."

"Or just cold," he pointed out. "I wouldn't have asked you to stay if you were in my way, and we're together most nights anyway. I know how the market is here and you don't have a lot of options, so you can crash here as long as you need to."

"Okay, I think I just feel..."

"Like you're used to doing things alone?"

"It's scary how fast you adapt to being on your own. I mean, I have my family and friends and all, but that's not the same as having a partner in life, you know?"

"Yeah, I do know. And I never took the plunge and tried the whole marriage thing, anyway."

"How come?" I had never pointblank asked him why he had remained a bachelor, but he also wasn't old enough for it to be a foregone conclusion. Early thirties was hardly past time to cross the possibility of matrimony off the list.

He shrugged. "It just hasn't worked out for me yet. I've spent all of my adulthood either working on my business or hunting vampires—hardly makes me relationship material."

"Screw that. You're a great catch."

"You've always had a way with words," Gabe grinned. "Tell

175

you what... Let me take this suitcase upstairs and you can unpack whenever you want. We'll make dinner and scour the online listings for a possible place for headquarters."

"I'll make dinner since you made breakfast," I said. He started to protest, but I overruled. "No, if I'm going to be here indefinitely, then I intend to contribute. Besides, I wanna give your fancy kitchen a test drive."

By the time we finished eating the grilled cheese sandwiches and tomato bisque I had pulled together—comfort food on a cold evening—we had located three properties that looked promising as temporary Amasai headquarters.

"We can go drive by and scope them out tomorrow," Gabe said. "But I doubt anyone will be around to let us in on Christmas Eve, so we'll just have to be patient."

"I'll be ready to have us all back under one roof. It doesn't feel right not to have a place for us all to be together."

"We will be. And I have some pull with a few building crews around here... Once we break ground on the new place, it won't take long to complete," my partner reassured.

I checked my watch. "It's still early yet. I feel like we should stay awake for a while in case Stacey catches something going on."

"I think so, too, but let's unplug. The last few days have been a lot to take in. How about a movie?"

"Something funny," I said.

"Something Christmas-y?" Gabe said at the same time.

We both laughed at how quickly we had narrowed the pool.

"If we're talking Christmas and funny, there's one that stands the test of time," he said.

"National Lampoon's."

"Bingo. I have it on digital, if you wanna look it up. I'll go

176

make popcorn."

I snagged the remote control off the coffee table and navigated to the menu that showed the movie library. And library was no exaggeration. He had enough film fare to rival my own, and in far more genres.

"Between your movie collection and mine, I think we could cover the entire modern film era."

Gabe laughed from the kitchen as he opened and shut the microwave door. "I don't have time for TV—it's too much of an investment to keep up with episode after episode."

I found what we were looking for and selected it from the search results. Since it had a lengthy musical intro, I started it as the first pops started up in the kitchen. It only took a few bars of the cheerful Christmas music to take me back to watching it with my family every year as far back as I could remember. It had always been one of Grandpa Fred's favorites, even though Grandma Hattie had decried the amount of language in it. As an adult looking back, I wondered if she opposed the occasional f-bomb on principal only since she laughed the entire way through the movie every time.

Gabriel returned to the living room just in time with not only a huge bowl of popcorn but more of the hot cocoa like the night before. We fell into a pleasant rhythm of munching and sipping and laughing at the hilarious absurdity of Chevy Chase's antics. The humor was the perfect antidote to the troubles of the week, easing some of the burden that came with hurts and anxiety.

And even vampires must not like to be caught out in winter storms because we never heard from Stacey that night.

Chapter 19

"It looks like it's pretty busy inside. Why don't I just drop you off, and I'll run over to my office to grab that paperwork, that way you can get us a table. I won't be long."

"Yeah, good idea. I wouldn't have expected it to be so packed today."

Gabe dropped me off right at the door, so I didn't have far to go in the cold. I stomped my boots on the rug just inside the door to knock off the snow that had accumulated in those few steps, just as it seemed others had done before me since there were soggy spots and still-melting snow on it.

There was one empty table in the whole place—a booth against the far wall. Bobby Sue smiled when she spotted me and asked how many of us there would be. She grabbed a pair of menus and two sets of rolled silverware, and waved me over to the open table.

"It's hopping in here today," I said as I sat and shrugged out of my coat.

"This is about the time folks get tired of cooking so much at home every year. Coffee for you today?"

"Yes ma'am, as usual. Two, please."

"I'll be right back with those."

I was looking at the menu—not that I needed it—when I thought Gabe slid into the seat across from me.

"I think I'm gonna have the loaded omelet. What about you?" I asked without looking up.

"I hear the pancakes are good."

That deep voice had me simultaneously taking a sharp look up and reaching for the handgun at the small of my back.

"What the hell do you think you're doing?" I seethed.

"Pleading my case," Creed said. "I figured I shouldn't press my luck without being in full view of witnesses."

"You figured right."

"Gonna shoot me right here in front of all these people?"

"I haven't decided yet."

My hand hadn't moved from the grip on the gun. Just like the first time we had met—maybe I should've taken that as a sign.

Creed laughed and flashed me a grin. I ground my teeth together and wondered how I had ever found his confidence attractive, especially when it bordered on arrogance. Also not unnoticed by me was that said swagger had reappeared, though I was none the wiser as to why.

"That's what I love about you. I'm not sure you wouldn't put a bullet in me right here and now."

I glanced around the diner at the other patrons, none of whom were paying attention to the tense exchange in the back booth. They were just grateful for a break in the weather and somewhere to eat on Christmas Eve that wasn't home.

I pinned Creed with a hard look. "Let's get something straight. You and me? Not happening. No matter what you say here, it changes nothing."

"Valan is helping me find my father."

My breath left my lungs in a rush. There were so many things wrong with that statement, I didn't know where to start. I landed on the question of what Valan was getting in return for his help. Because there was something.

"Why?" was the only thing that came out.

"Why?" he repeated. "Why not?"

"What, like you want a list?" I fired back. "First, he's using you somehow. Second, you claim to love me but fall in line with my mortal enemy at first chance, and I'm supposed to be good with that?"

Creed interrupted before I could get any farther down my extensive list. "Valan isn't your enemy."

"Bullshit."

More with the arrogant laughing. If I made it through the exchange without knocking his sparkling teeth in for all to see, it'd be my lucky day.

"So was it real? You, me—any of it?" I asked, even though I was afraid of the answer.

"At first, no. Eden and I were always out for ourselves. But when I kissed you—that first time when you slapped me—that was real. By then, I really did want you. And I wanted to do right by you."

I thought back to that first kiss, when he'd taken what I wasn't offering. They say people will show you who they are if you'll pay attention. Oh, how I wished I would have paid attention then.

The bells on the diner's main door jingled, drawing my attention.

Gabriel.

I watched his expression shift from a polite smile for Bobby Sue to a flinty look that could shrink the balls of Lucifer himself.

He was across the floor and toe-to-toe with Creed before

anyone else knew what was happening. I finally let go of my gun when I stood to be at my partner's side.

"Isn't it exhausting being the white knight all the time?" Creed drawled.

"I manage," Gabe gritted without giving an inch.

"So I guess right about now is when you tell me to take a hike."

"That's up to her," my partner said, tilting his head toward me.

"Right. Hide behind Remi. Like always," Creed grinned.

I balled up a fist, ready to wipe the stupid-ass expression clean off his face. But Gabe was there first, laying him out with a jab to the nose so quick I barely tracked it.

My mind wouldn't wrap around what my eyes were seeing. The man with a black belt in decorum and caution had Mayweathered Creed without hesitation.

In spite of myself, I had to stifle a laugh. While my ex-boyfriend (big, fat emphasis on the ex) made like a sack of taters on the diner floor, I covered my mouth with both hands. I looked at Gabriel, eyes wide.

"You okay?" I whispered.

"Never better," he said, shaking out his hand. "I've been wanting to do that for a while."

Every eye in the place had turned to us. How could they not? But since the altercation had ceased with the one blow, no one looked on in fear. Rapt fascination showed on all the faces turned toward us.

Gossip would circulate around Dove Creek even before all the Christmas presents had been opened the next morning.

Creed recovered his wits and swiped at the blood gushing from his nose. Lurching to his feet, there was a fight in his eyes.

One Bobby Sue promptly threw a wet blanket on.

"No sir, no you don't! Not in here. I know if *he* hit you, it was for good reason. So go bleed somewhere else, not on my floor," she ordered.

He was good and pissed off, but not stupid enough to try his luck while outnumbered in front of fifty strangers and a woman who would clock him with a cast iron skillet if he messed up her restaurant.

"We could've really been something if you weren't so wrapped up in being a hero for this town, in the Amasai, in... *him*," he spat.

We'd need all day to argue everything that was wrong about why we wouldn't be something. But I didn't have all day, so I went the straightforward route.

"Go to hell."

There was no irony in that statement since that was exactly where he was headed, throwing his lot in with Valan and the demons. It felt good saying it, small and petty though it was on my part.

Even more satisfying was watching him stalk out with his tail between his legs. I knew we weren't done with him. He wasn't going to run away after one hit *justlikethat*.

And he had to pay.

Using me was just the tip of the iceberg—I'd get over it, even faster now after what had just gone down. But for what he'd done to our headquarters, to Garret, and most of all to Hugo... He was on the wrong side of the line in the sand.

"Rem?" Gabriel's voice cut through my thoughts and I refocused to find him and Bobby Sue looking at me like they had been talking and expected an answer.

"I'm sorry—what did you ask?"

"I was just saying we should probably go, too."

"Yeah, you're right. I don't think I could eat after that, anyway," I agreed.

Gabe turned back to Bobby Sue. "We're sorry about all this. I don't think anything was damaged."

"Except that fool's ego," she laughed. "And don't worry about it. It'll be the talk of the town for a few days and folks will be lined up to get a firsthand account."

"We'll get out of your way for now, then," I said, eager to be out of the way of curious stares.

"I'll see you next time," Bobby Sue said firmly, as though ensuring we heard we were still welcome.

The bracing cold that had settled on Dove Creek was still a shock to the system after leaving the heated diner. I took a deep breath as my boots crunched on the hard-packed snow in the parking lot.

Gabe and I got in his car and while he fired it up immediately, we both just sat still for a moment.

"Tell me what you're thinking?" he asked.

"I know where this path leads. I know what he's going to force me into," I said.

We locked eyes, and he nodded to show he understood.

"I'm sorry I caused a scene in there," Gabe said.

I scoffed. "Are you kidding me? I was gonna hit him myself if you hadn't gotten there first."

"Then that's not what you're upset about."

"No way," I smiled. "I think I'm rubbing off on you."

"Maybe," Gabe smiled back. "But he asked for it."

"No doubt."

"Before we were so rudely interrupted, I was going to tell you some good news. Great news, actually."

"Oh? I could use some of that."

"When I was in my office, I got a call from Rusty Sumner. He had told his wife about our visit yesterday and she apparently guilted him into leasing us his place. Not so much as an extra deposit required."

I nearly cried, I was so relieved. "Thank God for nagging wives. When can we move in?"

"We sign the paperwork Friday and he's giving us the keys then."

The buzz of optimism lifted my mood. We would have a place to call home until our permanent new headquarters was built.

"Let's get something to eat. We can get Miss Ginger's and take it home," he suggested.

We were still sitting in the parking lot of the diner, not going anywhere fast. He put the car in reverse and eased out. The bakery was a scant two blocks down from where we were and had a drive through with (score!) only one car waiting in it.

The aroma of cinnamon rolls and coffee filled the car, and my stomach roared in anticipation. I was even more grateful to Rusty Sumner since we could go straight to Gabriel's house to eat rather than check out more buildings.

"I was thinking… We usually have a get-together at HQ for Christmas. Since we can't do that this year, we can get everyone over to my place," Gabe said.

Even though no one would be in the mood for a real party, it was a tradition that should be upheld.

"That's a great idea. If there's ever a time we should all be together, it's now."

He pulled carefully into the driveway and brought the car slowly to a halt to avoid a skid.

"Agreed. We'll keep it low-key. And make it potluck. I don't think we can manifest Christmas dinner for fifteen with what's in the fridge."

I laughed. "Not likely."

Chapter 20

After the indulgent breakfast and a day spent doing some strategic planning with Gabriel, I was feeling much more even-keeled than when we had left Bobby Sue's after the run-in with Creed. In hindsight, it was almost a mental load off to know I hadn't been completely taken in—he had had true feelings for me, even if he didn't go into it with that intention.

I got ready for the Christmas Eve family party at my mom's and ended up looking more festive than I felt. Which was for the better; I would avoid a motherly interrogation that way.

Downstairs, I found Gabriel at the dining room table with a set of building plans rolled out before him and a steaming cup of hot tea to one side. Glasses on, he studied a tiny detail and marked something in pencil.

"Are you sure you don't want to come with?" I asked him. "You'd be more than welcome."

With all of the snow we had gotten, he had decided it was too risky to make the trip to Fort Worth and back to be with his family. Not that he was at all broken up about it, but I hated for him to be alone on Christmas Eve.

He looked up from his work. "I'm sure, thank you. I'm in for a quiet evening."

Then again, he and I had been spending every waking moment together for the last few days. Maybe alone was what he needed.

"Is this what you got from your office this morning?" I asked.

"Yeah, do you want to take a look before you go?"

I circled around to his side of the table to take a peek at the work he had brought home and recognized what it was. The blue lines intersecting and paralleling each other across the expansive white sheet formed the floor plan for our new headquarters.

"This is amazing," I told him.

Everything from the common area to the armory would be under one roof. There was nothing more and nothing less than exactly what we needed.

"I wish I could stay and admire it longer," I said.

"There will be plenty of time later. Nice dress, by the way."

I mirrored his smiling expression. "This old thing?"

The emerald green velvet wasn't old at all. I had scored it at a boutique in Creek Crossing when Jocelyn had gotten me out of my comfort zone a few weeks before. I had made it season- and action-appropriate by donning leggings and boots instead of the nylons and heels fashion would have dictated.

"And you're armed?" Gabe asked.

I simply cocked an eyebrow. *Duh.*

"Call me if anything weird happens."

"Always do. And don't worry... I'm going straight there and back, and I'll be home before curfew."

He shook his head at me and winked. "Get outta here."

I pulled on my coat and shook a tail feather getting out to the truck. The highway between Dove Creek and Westview had been plowed, so I wasn't slowed down much. Dylan and Joss were unloading presents from the backseat of his truck when I parallel parked at the curb.

"Heya, Rem."

"Merry Christmas!" Jocelyn called.

They both waved me over, and I got the gifts I had brought out of the passenger seat of the truck and dashed up the shoveled sidewalk.

"Hey, y'all. Merry Christmas to you, too."

"You should've ridden with us," my brother told me.

I shrugged. "Thought I was gonna talk Gabe into coming with."

"Let's get inside," Joss said, bouncing from foot to foot on her cute pumps. "It's freezing."

Mom and Hadden greeted us at the front door with smiles and hugs. It was cozy and warm inside, with a cheerful fire crackling in the living room fireplace. I stashed my gifts under the tree and took off my coat.

We were a small party but no less merry for it. James hadn't made the effort to come up for the Christmas Eve celebration for years, and this year he was falling back on the excuse of the bad weather. I was feeling less ungenerous toward him, however, after learning about the plea deal he was behind in the case against the Triple Six.

My mom cornered me at the coat rack when the others headed back to the dining room.

"You look beautiful, Remi-Jean," she said.

I smiled. "Thanks, Mom. Not tired, like always?"

"No. What changed?"

"Gabe and I have been taking it easy since the fire. We haven't been making rounds at night."

"I'm glad to hear it," she said. Backing off interrogation-mode, her tone softened. "I'm sorry about Creed."

"Don't be." When she looked like she would ask why, I added, "I'll tell you all about it later. Let's just enjoy ourselves tonight."

"You have a deal," she said, putting an arm around my waist as we went to the dining room. "Hadden made a ham that'll feed a small army."

I dwarfed my petite mother, so much so that I could give her shoulders a squeeze and kiss the top of her blonde head. Taking a seat across from Joss and Dylan, I noted the ham in the center of the table might not feed an army, but it and all the side dishes were far too much for the five of us.

"Mom's right—how many were you expecting?" I teased.

My mom's husband held his hands up in surrender, with the look of a man who aims to please his wife. "Lizzie always holds out hope James will come and bring his family. I cook accordingly."

"Well, I won't complain. I had enough leftovers after Thanksgiving to make turkey sandwiches for a week," Dylan grinned.

"Let's dig in, shall we?" Mom prompted.

There were a few minutes of 'pass the potatoes' while we all took helpings of what we wanted. When our plates were full, we paused to say grace before sampling Hadden's excellent cooking.

While there wasn't the buzz of excitement over opening presents like when we were children, there was a happiness and contentment in the air that was comforting. Jocelyn especially glowed from the inside out and seemed to enjoy the peace, given the position her sister and brother-in-law now found themselves in.

"When Gabe texted to invite us to his place tomorrow, he said y'all had found somewhere for us to use as a temporary

189

headquarters," Dylan said between bites.

I nodded. "We sign the paperwork Friday. We planned on telling everyone tomorrow."

"What's it like?" Joss asked.

"It's the big building Sumner Pipeline used to be in. It's still pretty new, and it's nice on the inside."

"It won't feel right," my brother said. "But I'm glad y'all found a place so fast."

"Me, too. Now if I only have that good luck finding myself a place," I said.

Mom put her fork down. "Do you really think Creed would try something if you stayed?"

I was deliberate in not siting the run-in at Bobby Sue's that morning as evidence that I had no idea what the hell his next move would be. Christmas Eve dinner was hardly the time to flop that ace onto the table.

"The truth is, I don't know what he'll do. But Gabe is putting me up for now and I appreciate being able to sleep with both eyes closed." I steered the conversation into more positive territory.

"That Gabriel really is the best of the Wyatt bunch," my mom said, picking up her fork again.

"That's not saying much," Dylan muttered. Joss goosed him in the ribs and he squawked. "What? Gabe deserves more credit than that."

Mom gave Jocelyn a knowing look before asking: "Who's ready for dessert?"

There was a collective groan about how full we all were, but no one refused. I got up from the table to help and collected the coffee cups while my mom got out the dainty plates she liked to use for dessert services.

"I truly do feel better with you having a safe place to stay," she said. "You know you're always welcome here, if you need."

"I know, Mom. And I appreciate it. But I don't want to be out of Dove Creek."

"I assumed as much. The offer stands nevertheless."

We took the dishes to the dining room, then went back for the pair of pies and coffee decanter. There was a coconut cream with perfect merengue, which was Dylan's favorite. And an apple pie with beautiful lattice over the top for me. Our mother had upheld the tradition for as many Christmases as I could remember—yet another comfort in a sea of tumultuous circumstances.

I poured coffee for everyone while our mom neatly sliced the pies and passed around what we each chose. There was more murmuring about how full we were, but how the pies were worth the misery. It was Jocelyn who returned us to actual conversation.

"So, what are the long-term plans for our headquarters?" she asked, dabbing her lips with a napkin. "Or is there a plan yet?"

"There is a plan, I can tell you that much. But we're going to tell everyone tomorrow night when we're all together," I said.

"No spoilers?" Dylan asked, hopeful I'd divulge a clue.

I shook my head. "No spoilers."

"You're no fun," my brother groused.

Since he was as good at sharing information as the middle-aged women who formed the branches of the town gossip tree, I knew the announcement would be as good as made if I revealed anything to Dylan.

I grinned at him as I left my seat to help clear the table.

"Let's just get all this to the kitchen for now and clean up later," Mom said. "We should go open our gifts."

Joss and Dylan shared a private smile, and I looked away to give them their moment, whatever it might've been about. The pang of being a singleton once more was still sharp, though it had been dulled somewhat by Creed's cowardly exit.

And burning our headquarters.

And stalking me in the diner.

Sick bastard.

I was better off without him, obviously. If I had to choose between an arrogant con or singlehood, yeah, sign me up to be alone for life.

It wasn't him I missed—it was all the things that come along with being a couple. Like secret smiles, as Jocelyn and my brother reminded me.

"Alright there?" Hadden tapped me on the shoulder since I was blocking the entrance to the kitchen.

I blinked and continued to the sink with the dirty plates in my hands. "Yeah, sorry. Think I had too much to eat."

He put the mostly full dishes of mashed potatoes and green bean casserole on the counter and turned toward me.

"I've never said so, but I hope you know I'm here for you, just like your mother is. You're a grown woman and God knows you don't need a father figure—and I'd never presume I could replace the one you lost. But I love Lizzie with all my heart and by extension I care for her family. I care for you."

My eyes teared up at the sentiment, and I gave him a quick, hard hug around the neck.

"I love that you love my mom. Maybe I am too old for all that step-parent stuff, but I know you're a friend to me."

"So, if you ever need an old guy's perspective, I'm all ears."

I laughed. "I'll keep that in mind. Right now, I'm just working through some things. I really will be okay."

"I know you will. If there's anyone who'll land on her feet, it's you—you get that from your mom."

"What's the hold-up, you two? Not doing those dishes, are you?" my mom asked as she burst into the kitchen.

"Speak of the devil and she shall appear," Hadden said, lips turning up in a wry smile.

"I heard that, mister! Now get a move on. Joss and Dylan are waiting."

When we got to the living room, Hadden crossed to the fireplace and added another log. It wasn't needed for warmth, what with central heat and air being added when the vintage house was remodeled, but it added to the coziness of the room.

At each of our feet, there was a small group of presents to unwrap. Since we were well into adulthood, it was more about quality over quantity, but no less fun than when we were kids.

We took turns tearing into wrapping paper and ooh-ing and ahh-ing over each well-chosen gift. I got a designer sweater from my mom that I was almost certain Jocelyn picked out because it was a pretty shade of cream, and both of them always complained that I wore too much black. But Mom and Hadden had also gotten me a gift card to my favorite archery shop, so I didn't complain in the least.

I picked up a flat, rectangular box from Joss and Dylan, but didn't get far with the paper before my brother stopped me.

"Wait! Mom needs to open hers from us at the same time."

I stopped what I was doing and waiting for our mother to pick up a box that was identical to mine. She and I exchanged curious looks, then smiled.

"Okay, I'm ready. Go!" she said.

We both ripped off the paper, which revealed plain white boxes. The tape easily gave way, and I found a shirt nestled inside tissue paper. I held it up to read the screen-printed words.

My mom gasped at the same time I did.

MY FAVORITE PERSON CALLS ME AUNTY

I clasped the shirt to my chest and shrieked with joy. "I don't believe it!"

"It's early days yet," Joss cautioned. "But we thought now was the best time to let our families know."

All five of us got to our feet and hugged as many tears of joy were wiped away. I would finally be an aunt in every sense of the word—I'd get to be involved. The excitement was overwhelming.

"I'm so happy for you," I told Jocelyn. "Have you told Meredith and Hugo?"

"Not yet. We're going to visit at the hospital tomorrow and we'll tell them then."

"We'll get you out of the rotation immediately. Actually, Dylan will need a new partner again, so he and Casey can pair up."

"I was thinking I'd stay in until I get bigger. You know, when I'm too big to move quickly."

I shook my head. "No way, not worth it. We won't put you at risk."

"But we're so short on people now. No Hugo, after losing Creed. Now if I have to step away, it only makes things tighter," she argued.

"So they'll be tighter. We'll deal. We'll go back to going on watch individually if we have to."

"I still feel bad."

"Don't. That little life is more important than anything," I told her.

She smiled and nodded, her blonde curls catching the light

and illuminating her already incandescent radiance. I had always heard pregnant women glowed, but in her case it seemed to be less about the biology of her situation and more about pure joy. Or maybe those things went hand-in-hand.

Her second chance at love, happiness, her own little family had come along in true, ideal fashion. I found myself hoping for my own second chance.

"We're moving up the wedding, by the way. I want to get it done before I'm showing. Not that I care what anyone thinks, but I want to look good in my dress for pictures."

That was the Jocelyn we all knew and loved.

I grinned. "You'll be gorgeous no matter what. When do we go dress shopping?"

"Soon… I was thinking we could go to Dallas right after…" she trailed off and eyed me with suspicion. "Wait. Did you just volunteer to go shopping?"

I waved off her who-are-you-and-what-have-you-done-with-Remi? "This is different—it's a big deal."

Just then, my brother appeared and pulled me into a crushing side hug. "What do you think, Rem? I'm gonna be a dad!"

Chapter 21

The back roads were empty as I took the long way home from Westview. Dirty snow piled up in the ditches on either side, but the asphalt was mostly clear from all the comings and goings of holiday merry-makers. And for the first time in days, the sky was clear, stars twinkling bright enough to rival the strings of lights that decorated the houses.

All the excitement about my brother and Jocelyn becoming parents re-routed my train of thought to our dad. He, Maria Vega, and David Lansing had begun the Amasai only the year before he and my mother found out they were expecting me. It felt a little like history repeating itself since it had been mere months since Dylan joined us, but I knew he'd let nothing come between him and his new little family.

The two-lane road took me around the lake and on to the edge of town where the Amasai headquarters had stood for nearly thirty years. I had told myself I was taking the long way to Gabriel's so I could savor the beautiful night, but as I slowed to a halt in front of the skeleton of our farmhouse, I wondered if it was an excuse put up by my subconscience.

Since I had told Gabe I was coming straight back, I didn't park and get out. Oddly, a pervasive sense of hope took me as I gripped the steering wheel. Even with everything that had been thrown at us from the destruction at our Dove Creek shop, the dead being unleashed, and now our very home being destroyed, we were still a family. A chosen family. The Amasai were still fighting together, side-by-side no matter the threat.

We would rebuild. I shifted into gear and continued on my way, eager to see more of Gabe's plans for our new HQ. Christmas seemed like a fitting time to tell the others and I hoped they would take the same comfort in having a plan of action as I did.

I passed the old school building just inside the town limits, the brick shell a perpetual reminder of the fiery conflict with the Triple Six that had ended in my father's death.

I always tried not to look at it, but in that moment, I was drawn to it, some nagging thought in the back of my mind fighting for purchase but not quite breaking through. An odd sense of deja vu.

It was befuddling enough that it caused me to slow my speed, but I didn't stop. I made up my mind to go chew on it some more and maybe talk it through with Gabriel. Giving air to what I was thinking and trying to get a grip on seemed like it would help. There was something about that place I had tried to ignore for months.

If I hadn't slowed down to get a grip on my musings, I would've missed it. There, in one of the fingers of the creek, a shadowy figure against the backdrop of pristine snow.

Hellhound.

I whipped into the parking lot and threw the truck into park. In hurried shorthand, I texted Gabe to get there pronto—the same place we had set up for the face-off with the Triple Six.

Shucking the heavy coat I wore, I braved the cold in favor of being able to move freely. In the reflex of routine, I had my quiver on my back with my bow snapped to it and a pair of forties loaded with silver bullets in my hands in a matter of seconds. Gabe had hit me back, letting me know he was on his way, so I took off across the empty lot.

I intended only to track the hellbeast, but as I covered ground and closed in, I saw the body it was dragging. My partner would be miffed if I took it on alone, but if there was the faintest chance the person was still alive, I had to take it.

Through the grove of bare oaks that stood between the creek and the school, I didn't have a clear shot. At that distance, I couldn't trust that the Holy Light would be effectual. I stayed in the lee of the gulley created by the creek bed, keeping myself in shadow and out of any wind. The water was at a slow trickle, just this side of freezing and low enough that I had plenty of room to stay in the dry.

My chance came when I reached a clearing in the trees at the same time the hellhound came to it above me. I scaled the side of the embankment to come up behind the beast and aimed. To be safe, I fired twice, both silver rounds finding their mark in the tough skull. It dropped into the snow with a great rumble.

I kept my guns trained on the hound as I approached, heaven forbid I had only wounded the thing. But there was no sign of life whatsoever, confirming the silver had done its job.

With the hellhound out of commission, I turned my attention to the body and hoped I was finding someone still living and breathing. They were still in the grip of the powerful jaws, facedown in the snow. I took a deep breath and reached in to pry apart both sides of that disgusting maw. Wrenching hard, I was able to free the person's neck and shoulder. Carefully, so I didn't cause any more damage, I turned the body over onto its back and gasped.

Bobby Sue.

Taking her wrist in my fingers, I checked for a pulse and found one. It was there, faint and unsteady, but she was still alive. I sent Stacey a text telling her to send an ambulance.

In my distraction, I forgot to keep an eye on my six.

The fanged nightmare grabbed me around the throat and hauled me up.

"Well, if it isn't the little bitch who shot me and left me to suffer."

Not Valan, then. Far too brutish and not nearly loquacious enough.

It sounded like the first one Gabe and I had left in the woods the night we toe-to-toed it with the hellhounds. The demon dog-walker carried a grudge.

I summoned the Holy Light to disseminate throughout my body, repelling the vampire. He let go of me and before I had the chance to hit him with a fatal dose of pure light, I heard the string of a crossbow sing.

In a split second, the shaft and fletching of the bolt protruded from his chest. The host body disintegrated to dust as the demon soul was drawn back to Perdition.

Gabe lowered his bow, chest pumping from the exertion of racing through the stand of trees.

"It's Bobby Sue!" I said frantically.

He ran the rest of the way over. "Is she alive?"

"Barely. I asked Stacey to call for an ambulance."

Meg and Gio came sprinting toward us and skidded to a stop next to Gabe and me. They shifted into their human forms.

"We scented the bloodsucker, then heard the gunshots," Meg said.

I nodded. "I just happened to cross paths with this thing. I

199

didn't see any others."

"We killed another of the hellhounds on the west side of the lake," Gio told us.

"I heard you when I was leaving," Gabe said. "You sounded close."

I looked at my partner and he gave a quick nod to show he knew what I was wondering. Had that hound been meant for one of us? Looking at Bobby Sue's prone form, I suspected Creed was sending a message.

The gloves were off.

Blue and red flashing lights filtered through the trees as the ambulance parked in the lot where I had left my truck.

"I'll go lead them in," Gabe said.

"We'll shift back and make ourselves scarce, but we'll be nearby until you're clear," Meg told me.

"Thank you both."

Gabe returned moments later with Brooke and her partner, Grady. Their rig had been wracking up frequent flier miles with the Amasai that week. As much as I liked the pair of paramedics, I didn't like seeing them that often. We exchanged a quick greeting and they got right to work.

"Was it this... *thing* that bit her?" she asked.

"Yes. It was dragging her, I don't know for how long before I found her."

"She's lucky you did."

They had her strapped to a stretcher and lifted her between the two of them.

"Can we be of any help?" Gabe asked.

"Just watch our backs til we get her out of here, if you don't mind."

"Not at all," I answered.

My partner and I flanked them as they carried Bobby Sue to the ambulance, Meg and Gio not within sight but no doubt watching out for us. We made it without incident, but we lingered there until Brooke and Grady were loaded up and speeding away.

When the flashing blue and reds were out of sight, Gabriel turned toward me. "You're okay? What the hell happened?"

"I'm fine. I'm sorry I didn't wait for you, but when I saw that thing dragging someone—"

"Don't apologize. You did the right thing. It's such a lucky break for Bobby Sue, I hate to think about the alternative."

I shivered from the cold and coming down from the adrenaline. "Let's get out of the open. I'll tell you all about it when we get to your place."

Gabe opened my door for me and stepped back. "You're right. Let's go."

We both had a gun in our hand when we got out of our vehicles at his townhouse. He had pulled into the garage and came out to help get my things and walk me inside.

Not a word passed between us about it, but with the were-wolves having killed a hellhound nearby, we were on our guard.

"Coffee?" Gabe asked once we were inside the safety of his house, doors locked.

I stowed my bow and quiver in the coat closet he used for weapons. "No, thanks. I'm gonna try to get some sleep after we're done talking."

"Herbal tea, then? I left everything out earlier."

"Perfect."

Following him to the kitchen, I perched on one of the tall chairs at the raised countertop. I glanced at the Christmas gift bag that held my presents from my mom's—Gabe had set it to one side, and I thought about the shirt inside from Jocelyn and my brother. They weren't telling everyone yet, but Gabe would need to know if we were keeping her out of the rotation.

I made up my mind to talk to her about it the next day and allow them to share their news as they saw fit. One day wouldn't affect our ability to plan so much that I had to tell him.

"I was coming the long way back," I said, turning my attention to Gabe in the kitchen. "I do that a lot when I'm coming home from my mom's. This weird feeling came over me when I was going past the school—it made me slow down. About the time I had made up my mind to come talk it over with you, I spotted the hellhound."

"What was the weird feeling?" Gabe asked, pouring hot water over the tea infusers. "Do you think it was you sensing the hellhound?"

"No, that was just dumb luck. It was something about the school itself... I felt this sort of deja vu or like I was supposed to remember something. But I was also thinking about my dad, so maybe it was just that."

I studied a dark vein in the granite, tracing it across the countertop.

"Don't be too quick to dismiss it. If there's one thing we know for certain, it's that this town works in mysterious ways. Honey?"

I looked up. "I'm sorry, what?"

"Do you want honey in your tea?"

"Oh, yes, please."

I watched him remove the tea balls from each clear mug, the water now a mellow shade of amber. As he stirred in the honey, I considered what he'd said about not dismissing what I had felt. He was right—when Dove Creek gave you a gut feeling about something, you had better pay attention.

"Want to take these to the living room?" Gabe asked.

"Yeah, definitely," I said, getting off the pub chair. "I wanna look out the windows and savor the sight of a white Christmas."

"We might get more snow later tonight."

"Really? The sky was so clear earlier."

He set a mug in front of me on the coffee table. "I was watching the ten o'clock news when you texted me. The weather guy said there's a strong chance after midnight."

I took the cup of tea Gabe had brought me and held it in both hands, warming them. It smelled of lavender and chamomile, a relaxing scent even in the most fraught times.

"Did you notice the vamp that attacked you was an older one?" he asked. "Went right to dust when I shot him. That has been getting more and more rare lately."

"Y'know, I don't think I fully thought about it," I sipped the tea. "He was the one who I shot in the gut that time when we first fought the hellhounds, but him being older would explain his healthy fear of Valan…"

My words trailed off while my thoughts raced ahead. An old vampire… The hellhound delivering a body… The sense of a nagging memory… My dad dying only a few yards from that place, demon possessed.

You do not realize it, but the place is familiar to you.

"The school," I whispered. "It's inside the school."

The altar where the Triple Six performed their summoning… Now all the dead bodies and rituals made sense. Their attempts to summon Apollyon failed because his demon form couldn't stay in the Mortal Plane for that long without a host. With my dad, at the abandoned elementary school, they had finally succeeded because they were at ground zero.

I burst from my seat and went to the windows. "I know where the Crossroads is."

"You... what? None of the algorithms showed us anything."

Turning away from the snow darkness, I looked at Gabe. "It's in the old school where the Triple Six raised Apollyon. Where that hellhound was dragging Bobby Sue tonight."

My partner appeared to mull over the revelation. He put down his mug and pinched the bridge of his nose between his thumb and forefinger. The silence stretched out for a solid minute.

"People said for years that place was haunted," he finally said. "Do you remember? When we were in school, so many odd occurrences. It got so bad, they didn't even move the furniture out of it when the new school was built."

"The library... That library was the worst. I remember it would get so cold, so fast you could—"

"See your breath in front of you," Gabe said at the same time. "That was what they made into the music room, thinking it might help."

"Right where the Triple Six..."

"Yeah."

Our eyes locked as we fell back into contemplative silence. Gabe was coming around to understand what I felt.

"Your gut is usually right. I don't care about the hard data. I trust your instincts on this," he said.

I beamed. "Thank you. Now, let's go check it out."

"Hold up," Gabriel said, holding both hands palm out. "We can't go just the two of us, at night. If that situation with the hellhound was what you suspect, there's no telling what we might walk into."

My shoulders slumped, but I agreed. My partner's caution

was well-founded. It wouldn't do us a whole hell of a lot of good to find the Crossroads, only to get killed—or worse, having our own souls replaced with demons'—for running in half-cocked.

"You're right," I told him. "I don't really want to slow my roll, but I think it could get ugly if we just waltz right in there."

"Let's get past Christmas, then we'll go in at dawn with the whole team. What's left of us," he tacked on.

I didn't mention that Joss wouldn't be in our number. He'd find out soon enough. Our manpower was taking a serious nosedive.

"And we'll just see what we see?"

"For the time being, yes. The fact is, even if your hunch proves correct, we don't know how to close the breech between Planes."

"Michael told me we have every tool we need at our disposal." I moved away from the windows and sat back down on the couch. "What do you think that means?"

Gabe shook his head. "I'm not sure. It could have to do with the abilities Yescha gave us. They didn't tell you anything else?"

"No. They're forbidden from getting involved. Can't interfere with the divine balance, or something like that. But if *we* tip the scales, all on our own—"

"All bets are off."

"You got it."

Chapter 22

Everyone was coming—every person from the Amasai, plus Meg and Gio were coming to our impromptu Christmas get-together. Even Solomon planned to look in after he was off duty. The holiday is some kind of lightning rod for domestic crimes, so it was all hands on deck for the local law enforcement; otherwise, he said, he would have come for the entire evening.

We had mentioned the party to Meredith when we visited the hospital that morning, but didn't press her with an invitation since she was spending all her free time with Hugo at the hospital. They promised to do a video call, though, to wish us all a Merry Christmas.

Gabriel and I had divulged my hunch and our plans to Hugo during that morning's visit. We told him the backstory and about Bobby Sue. He had seemed invigorated by the prospect of shutting down the demons' source of entry, but offered no guidance. I wondered if he didn't have anything additional for us to consider, or if he was holding back to give us room to lead the mission as we saw fit.

We were also able to get an update about Bobby Sue's condition from her family. She couldn't yet have visitors outside immediate family members, but it looked like she would pull through. The flowers we left felt like a poor offering in comparison to what she had been through. She was, after all, targeted because she was a friend to us.

Survivor's guilt crashed over me like a wave as I looked at my reflection in the mirror. There I was putting on lipstick and fussing over my pretty new sweater while two people lay in hospital beds. It felt all wrong.

I went downstairs and found Gabriel with his remote control built for world dominance, setting the lights to the exact right level.

He turned when he heard my footsteps. "You look very..." paused, cleared his throat. "Festive."

"Thanks," I said. Looking down at the sweater, I added, "My mom gave this to me last night."

"It's perfect. But what's wrong?"

"How do you know something's wrong?"

Gabe said nothing—the eyebrow raise I got did all the talking.

"It's just that I feel terrible being here and enjoying ourselves while other people can't," I shrugged. "Kinda stupid, I know."

"Not stupid at all. But us sitting around being miserable and feeling guilty won't help them."

"I know, but I feel weird about it all... especially stepping into Hugo's place, you know? Doing things he would normally do. Taking on his responsibilities all while he's laid up in a hospital bed."

"He asked us to do these things—this is what he intended, whether because he chose retirement or was forced out by injury, or... worse. You didn't shove him out of the way."

"Of course not, I would never—I thought I could do it. When Hugo stepping away was just a hypothetical, it made sense. I'm a legacy member, after all. Now, though, I'm not as sure."

Gabe shook his head. "This isn't about your dad, Rem. It's about you and what you're capable of. Hugo sees it... I see it." He put his hands on my upper arms with a reassuring squeeze. "We're a team. I can't do this without you. I *won't* do this without you."

I opened my mouth to respond, then shut it again when I couldn't find the words. Before I could continue with the fish-out-of-water routine, the doorbell rang, and Gabriel looked like no one regretted it more than him.

He went to answer the door and returned with Joss and Dylan. My brother carried a huge crock-pot full of something that smelled delicious, and Gabe accompanied him to the kitchen to set it up. Jocelyn met me in the living room.

"I'm so glad you like the sweater," she said. "I helped your mom pick it out, but she has great taste herself."

The confirmation of my suspicions made me smile. "She does. And I've always been a disappointing shopping partner for her, so I'm glad she has you now."

"There's one big shopping trip coming up that I hope you're ready for."

"Dress shopping?"

"Yup. Girls day, Dallas, in two weeks. I've already asked Meredith, and she said she'd be okay leaving Hugo by then. The two of you are my only bridesmaids, so finding something for both of you ought to be easy."

"I'll be there. What colors did you settle on?"

The question rolled off my tongue without a second thought. Having a growing enthusiasm for discussing wedding plans was something that surprised me. And it was a good time to be pleasantly surprised by something.

"Navy and blush. It's close to Valentine's Day, so I want to avoid all the cliches."

Dylan and Gabriel emerged from the kitchen, chatting about the place we Amasai would be moving into at the end of the week.

"Have you told him yet?" Joss asked quietly.

When I looked confused, she pointed at her still-flat stomach.

"Oh, right. No, I haven't said anything."

"Said anything about what?" Gabe asked.

"Well... We have news. I'm pregnant!" She beamed as she shared her sweet secret.

Gabriel hugged Jocelyn and congratulated her, then clapped palms with Dylan.

"We aren't telling everyone just yet, but you need to know because Remi and Dylan decided last night that I'm out of the nightly rotation."

"They're right," he agreed.

"And I want to ask you to be a groom's guy... thing. In the wedding," Dylan said.

"Groomsman," Joss and I both chimed in at the same time and giggled.

"It's going to be in February," she added.

"The date doesn't matter—I'm honored to be a part of your day," Gabe said.

The doorbell rang again, and I went to get the door so he could finish congratulating my brother and Jocelyn. I saw through the narrow window that it was quite a crew.

Matt and his wife Janine, plus Ty and Stacey, Aric and Garret all came out of the cold, most of them holding a dish or two. I let them get inside, then pulled Garret into a hug.

"I didn't expect you to make it. Are you feeling okay?" I asked him.

He pushed his thick glasses farther up his nose and nodded. "I'm mostly just tired now, like I'm getting over a bad respiratory infection."

"Come sit down then," I told him. "Don't wear yourself out."

I guided him to a comfy chair in the living room, close enough to be a part of the conversation, but out of the way so he didn't get bumped into.

"I'll get you something to drink," I offered.

"Nothing alcoholic, or I'll be blacked out until next Tuesday with all the meds I'm on," he said with a small smile.

I smiled back. "You got it."

Gabriel let Meg and Gio in while I made Garret a glass of sweet tea and took it to him. Not long later, Casey was the last to arrive and chips and queso and a case of craft beer. The party was complete, but it felt foreign not to have Hugo and Meredith among us.

Even with them missing from the group, it felt right for us to all be together.

Creed and Eden had tried to tear us apart from the inside—Eden with her own agenda, then Creed defecting to our enemies. He had destroyed our home, our place of refuge and safety, but he had not destroyed us.

I looked around at the people surrounding me and found that same sense of home I had always felt at the old farmhouse.

We would miss our original headquarters, it was true, but we would have a new place soon and we would make it home. As long as we held together, no one could stop us.

With the Sumner building soon to be ours, a strong hunch on where the Crossroads was located, and the promise of new life, my hope was renewed. I still wasn't keen on leading, but I had made Hugo a promise. And after all he'd done for me, I planned to make good on that vow.

Gabriel stepped away from the others and joined me in the corner of the room.

"I would ask if you're still feeling guilty about having our party, but you look happy just now."

I smiled at my partner. "I am happy. And you were right… We do all need to be together."

"Back when you first joined the Amasai and until not long ago, I never thought I'd hear you say those words," he said, smile matching mine. When I looked confused about which, he added, "You. Were. Right," like he was savoring them.

"Never is a long time," I laughed. "But we have come a long way."

"Merry Christmas, Remi."

"Merry Christmas."

About the Author

H. Anne Henry was born and raised in small-town north Texas, and often draws inspiration from the windswept landscape for many of the locales described in her books. When she isn't busy pecking away at a story, she spends time with her husband and three young sons. She can also be found squeezing in some time to read, trying out new recipes to feed her hungry crew, snapping photos, and exploring her new surroundings in San Angelo, Texas.

She is happy to connect with readers (and swap recipes!) on Facebook, Instagram, and Pinterest.

You can connect with me on:
- ⊕ https://hannehenry.com
- 🐦 https://twitter.com/H_AnneHenry
- 📘 https://www.facebook.com/hannehenry.author
- ⌀ https://www.instagram.com/h.annehenry
- ⌀ https://www.pinterest.com/HAnneHenryAuthor
- ⌀ https://www.goodreads.com/hannehenry

Subscribe to my newsletter:
- ✉ https://mailchi.mp/5ea4b92af9d2/ebook-backmatter